Sealed with a Secret

BY LISA SCHROEDER

SCHOLASTIC INC.

For Amanda and Sarah,

editorial duo extraordinaire.

Thank you so much for everything.

Copyright © 2016 by Lisa Schroeder

This book was originally published in hardcover by Scholastic Press in 2016.

All rights reserved. Published by Scholastic Inc., *Publishers since 1920*. SCHOLASTIC and associated logos are trademarks and/or registered trademarks of Scholastic Inc.

The publisher does not have any control over and does not assume any responsibility for author or third-party websites or their content.

No part of this publication may be reproduced, stored in a retrieval system, or transmitted in any form or by any means, electronic, mechanical, photocopying, recording, or otherwise, without written permission of the publisher. For information regarding permission, write to Scholastic Inc., Attention: Permissions Department, 557 Broadway, New York, NY 10012.

This book is a work of fiction. Names, characters, places, and incidents are either the product of the author's imagination or are used fictitiously, and any resemblance to actual persons, living or dead, business establishments, events, or locales is entirely coincidental.

ISBN 978-0-545-90735-4

10 9 8 7 6 5 4 3 2 1   17 18 19 20 21

Printed in the U.S.A.   40
First printing 2017

Book design by Yaffa Jaskoll

Sealed
with
a
Secret

Chapter 1

CRICKET: A BAT-AND-BALL GAME

Paris is a wonderful city, it's true, but in my mind, there's no place better than London, and I was thrilled to be home. Homebody Phoebe Ainsworth, that's me. Give me a book to read, a piano, or a kitchen filled with gadgets, and I'm happier than a foodie in a five-star French restaurant. My older sister, Alice, however, was acting as if the world was coming to an end. She hadn't wanted to leave Paris. Well, that isn't exactly true. She hadn't wanted to leave *Justin*.

I sat on the edge of Alice's bed staring at the large fish tank across the room, trying to decide if I should be the nice sister and rub her back as she sniveled into her pillow. My parents gave Alice the fish tank for her fifteenth birthday. Mum had told her she'd read an article that said aquariums can help calm the mind and reduce stress. So they filled it with beautiful fish in the hopes that Alice's room would be become a relaxing, soothing place, even when she's anxious about school and grades. My sister is ambitious and, as Mum likes to say, a perfectionist with a capital *P*. Sometimes it seems like she lives in a constant state of worry. I never understood what she had to worry about, since she always gets good grades.

As I sat there next to her, I considered telling her to roll over and watch the fish, because maybe it would help her feel better. But I'm sure she would have told me it would definitely *not* help. Fish don't have magical powers to cure a wounded heart, after all. Though that'd be pretty cool if they did.

It'd been five days since we'd said farewell to our new American friends, Nora and Justin, whom we'd met while in Paris with our dad to look for antiques. But you wouldn't have known it by looking at my sister. It was like she and Justin had kissed good-bye only a moment ago.

It was Monday morning, and I'd come to her room to tell her I was making strawberry crêpes before we went with Dad to work at the antiques shop. Next thing I knew, she'd flopped down on her bed face-first.

The longer I sat there, the more irritated I became. All I wanted her to do was to join us for breakfast, and she was acting like the world was ending.

I stared at the fish, hoping they might make *me* feel calm. It didn't work.

"Let me guess," I finally said with a sigh. "Crêpes remind you of Justin. Well, you don't have to have any breakfast, you know. Go hungry if you'd like. I was just trying to be nice."

Of course I missed my new friend, Nora, too. But not enough to cry about it. After all, we'd only known each other for a few days, and from the moment we met on the Métro, I knew that our time together in Paris was temporary.

While Justin and Alice were off falling head over heels in love, Nora and I had gone on glorious adventures around the City of Light. Nora's grandmother had made up a treasure hunt for her, with items scattered in various places. We'd had so much fun together, but as

Mum liked to say from time to time, "All good things must come to an end." Besides, something told me I'd see Nora again someday. Maybe she would come to London, or maybe I'd travel to New York City, where she lived. That would be a dream come true! In the meantime, we'd stay in touch. I was sure of it.

And so, here we were, back at our flat in south London (Greenwich, to be exact) with another week of Easter holiday before we returned to school. If Alice intended to blather on about Justin the entire time, it was going to be one *very* long week.

"Cooxhughetmaatissh?" Alice mumbled, her head turned only slightly so the pillow heard her words better than I did.

"I'm sorry, I don't understand baby talk."

She sat up, sniffling. "I'm not a baby, Phoebe. I'm heartbroken. But, silly me, you wouldn't understand since you've never been in love." She dragged her arm across her nostrils. *Gross.* "I said, could you get me a tissue?"

"Why?" I asked. "Are your legs broken, too?"

She stood up with a harrumph. "You're not nice at all. In fact, you're the meanest little sister in the history of the world."

While she went toward the loo, I headed back to the kitchen. "Breakfast will be delicious and you'll regret not having any," I yelled. "All because of a silly boy."

Dad and Mum sat at the old, pedestal kitchen table, drinking tea and reading the newspaper. Our house is small and filled to the brim with antiques. If something doesn't sell at the store, I think Dad feels guilty, so he brings it home and pretends like it's something he really wanted to keep anyway. A few weeks ago, he tried to bring home an antique cricket bat.

"But you don't play!" Mum had cried.

"I might," Dad had told her. "Someday."

That's when Mum put her foot down and made Dad promise he wouldn't bring any more stuff home until he got rid of some things. I kind of agreed with her. I mean, what was next, a vintage coffin? I could just hear Dad's perfectly good reason—"I don't need it now, but someday I will."

I walked over to the stove and turned it on. Eyes were on me, I could feel it. Finally, Mum said, "Weren't you being a bit harsh with your sister, lovey?"

I let out an exasperated sigh. "She's too lovesick to eat breakfast. You can't tell me you think that's perfectly acceptable."

As the pan warmed, I dropped a pat of butter into it, which made a nice sizzling sound. I'd mixed up the batter before I went to Alice's room, but I took the wooden spoon and gave it a few quick turns to ensure it was nice and thin.

"It's a lucky thing the two of you are going with me to the shop today," Dad said, setting the newspaper down on the table. "There's nothing like a good day's work to take your mind off your troubles."

"Don't be surprised if she comes out here and says she's changed her mind about going," I said, swirling the pan around to get the bottom of it nicely covered with the butter.

Mum stood up and brought her teacup to the sink. "Well, she's going whether she likes it or not. I have a shift at the hospital and I don't want her moping about at home by herself all day long."

"Why does she have to be so impossible anyway?" I wailed. "I miss the old Alice. The one who used to sing along while I played the piano. The one who made sure I got the last biscuit during teatime. The one who loved to browse flea markets with me rather than going off on her own." I sighed. "You know, the one who actually *liked* being with me."

I leaned into my mother when she came over and put her arm around me. "She still likes you, Phoebe. This is only temporary. You'll see."

"I'm not so sure about that," I said as I went back to making breakfast. "You didn't see how she treated me in Paris. I couldn't do anything right. She wouldn't even let me sit next to her on the Métro. Although I suppose that turned out to be a good thing, since it allowed me to meet Nora."

While I poured the batter into the pan, Dad said, "What you two are going through is normal. Your sister is growing up, that's all. She's trying to figure out who she is. What she wants out of life."

"Or *doesn't* want out of life," I said as I watched the bubbles appear and took in the delicious aroma of the batter cooking. "Like her sister, for example."

Mum chuckled. "Sweetheart, don't you think you're being a bit overly dramatic?"

"Not really," I replied.

I flipped the thin pancake over and was happy to see it wasn't too dark, the way they usually turned out when Mum made them for us.

"Look at that," she said, peering over my shoulder. "You obviously didn't learn how to cook from me."

That was another thing Alice and I used to do together a lot—cook. Since Mum and Dad were pretty lousy at it, we'd taken it upon ourselves to do as much of the cooking as possible. And I loved doing it. Alice had taught me so much. Not just when it came to cooking, either. With six years between us, she'd often been more like a second mother to me than a sister.

But soon she'd be off to university, and then what? Once she left, would she even care to stay in touch with me at all?

"Let me get the strawberry jam," Mum said as she made her way to the fridge.

I had hoped Alice would change her mind and join us for breakfast after all. But she didn't. And as I went to work making another crêpe, no matter how wonderful they looked, I wished with all of my heart that I'd chosen something different to cook that morning.

Chapter 2

GOBSMACKED: AMAZED

After breakfast, I went into my room to finish getting ready to go to the shop with Dad and Alice. Instead of a fish tank in my room, there's a bulletin board filled with happy notes. When I got the board a few years ago for my birthday, I knew I wanted to do something special with it. So that first year, I decided to try to become a better artist. Every day I drew a picture on a notecard and hung it on the board. I thought it would be neat to see how much my artistic skills changed throughout the year. I was so happy to see at the end of 365 days that I had improved quite a bit. And I loved how the board looked when I was finished.

Last year I printed out recipes with pictures from the Internet once a week. I pinned up the picture, and then took the recipe to the kitchen and added the ingredients to the shopping list. Some of the recipes were good and others were . . . not. Like the tuna burgers I made? Blech.

Next, I came up with the idea for the happiness board. Now, as I stared at the big smiley face I'd drawn on a piece of paper, I smiled to myself. All around the smiley face were colorful notes of things that had made me feel happy. I think I'd been worried that this year would not be a very happy year, with Alice heading off to university in the fall. So I'd told myself it would be up to me to find things to be glad about.

For example, when I got back from Paris, I printed these words on a purple notecard:

I made a friend from New York while I was in Paris.
Her name is Nora.

Along with the note, I'd hung a picture of us that I'd taken as we'd climbed the Panthéon together. I'd snapped one with the breeze blowing our hair all around, her brown hair and my blonde hair mixed up together.

But it didn't matter that our hair was a little messy, because our faces said it all—we'd had a blast together.

As I looked at all of the colorful cards and the few photos I'd stuck up there, too, my heart told me I had a lot to be happy about. I needed to try not to let Alice and her teenage mood swings bring me down.

I turned my attention to the item I'd come to my room to get—a special treasure I'd found two days before we came home from Paris. Although Alice and I didn't know a lot when it came to hunting for special pieces, we did know to look for designer-named jewelry and other types of accessories—Tiffany, Cartier, Gucci, etc. When we'd split off from Dad to cover more ground, that's what Dad had asked Alice and me to look for, specifically.

Alice had been nearby, in another section of the flea market, when I happened upon a little black pouch with something inside. It didn't look like much, sitting in a small heap with all of the ugly costume jewelry. But when I went to examine the contents, I found a gold makeup compact with pretty little jewels on the outside. Ever so carefully, I turned it over in my hands, examining it closely, and when I saw the word *Cartier* in very tiny cursive letters near the front, where it opens, I think my heart skipped a beat.

I could not believe it.

My hands started shaking, and as much as I wanted to open it and see what was inside, I knew I had to stay calm and act like this was just some junky little trinket that had absolutely no value. And that might have been the case, because what did I know, really? Still, I had a feeling it was special.

"Ooh, *très magnifique!*" said a voice behind me. I whipped around to find a teen girl with short pink hair standing there. She must have been looking over my shoulder and I hadn't even realized it.

"It is, isn't it?" After I said it, I wondered if she spoke English. "*Parlez-vous anglais?*"

"*Oui.*" She stuck out her hand. "I'm Cherry. Pleased to meet you."

I took her hand and gave it a shake. "I'm Phoebe." I took a deep breath and gave her a weak smile. "And I'm quite nervous. I have to put on my sweet angel face."

She looked totally confused. "*Excusez-moi?*"

I leaned in and whispered, "It's a trick my sister taught me. Basically, I have to act like a sweet angel who doesn't know the first thing about bartering. I'm just an innocent kid who has found a worthless trinket. But it's tricky, you know? Because I *really* want it!"

"Ah, but of course," Cherry said with a smile. "That makes sense. So you are a good actress, yes?"

A memory flashed in my mind, of Alice and me, giggling frantically and running off when we'd been successful in getting a piece of Blue Willow china a few years back. Our parents had been given a set of the vintage china for their wedding, but it'd been missing a few key pieces. When Alice and I found the creamer at a flea market, we knew we had to try our best to get it for their wedding anniversary. That's when Alice taught me about the sweet angel face. I was gobsmacked as I watched her performance. When it was over, the man behind the counter gave her the creamer for a great price.

I looked at Cherry, telling myself if my sister could do it, I could, too. "I'm going do my very best." I smiled sweetly, batting my eyelashes a few times. "How's that?"

She giggled. "*Magnifique!* Oh, you know what else you must do? Wait and step up to barter when she is very busy. Because she will wish to hurry on with you, a young girl, who has little money."

"Oh, that's good advice. Thank you." I gulped as I slid the compact back into the little pouch. "I hope I can do this."

"You can and you will," she said confidently.

We stood and chatted about a vintage children's book she'd bought from a different vendor. Finally, after a number of customers had approached the vendor, talking and bartering, making the booth quite chaotic, Cherry gently pushed me toward the table. It was showtime.

I asked the elderly lady in charge of the booth if she spoke English. She shook her head, telling me no. I didn't know much French, but I held out the pouch like it was nothing, wearing my charming, innocent angel face the entire time. After I quickly asked how much she wanted for the item, I held my breath and waited to see if she would grab it from my hands to explore the contents. Lucky for me, someone else stepped up just then with a beautiful Victorian-style lamp, and offered a price for it. The vendor shook her head frantically and responded with a different number.

This was my chance. The vendor was now distracted, and that could only be good for me. I reached into my pocket and pulled out a ten-euro note. Dad had given me twenty total, but I figured I should start with ten. I smiled even wider as I held it out to her, wishing with all my might that she would take it without any further questioning.

The woman with the lamp scowled and came back with a counteroffer, speaking in rapid French. The vendor shook her head again, and snipped back at her, and as they went back and forth, I stood quiet and still, until finally, the old woman snatched the bill from my hand and shooed me away.

"*Merci*," I said before I turned around, and scurried off with Cherry at my heels.

"You did it!" she exclaimed when I finally stopped.

"I'm so excited!" I told her. "Thank you for being there and helping me through it."

"It was nothing. Now I must run to meet a friend. *Bonne journée!*"

My dad had told me once that means "have a good day."

"I will, thanks to you," I told her as she waved and scampered off into the crowd.

I'd stuffed the compact into the pocket of my peacoat and hadn't said a single word about it to Alice or

Dad. I'd wanted to wait until I could find out more about my discovery when we were back at home.

To keep my dad from getting suspicious, I'd purchased a simple vintage necklace later that morning with my remaining money. Of course I told Dad I'd spent the entire twenty euros on that piece alone. He hadn't questioned me about it at all, fortunately.

Today, I hoped to sneak away to see if we'd ever carried anything similar in our shop, and what the value of the compact might be. If it was worth a lot of money, and I had a feeling it was, I could be Alice's hero.

My family had been hoping for a small miracle—a spectacular find while we were in Paris to help with university costs for Alice. As I put the compact in my bag, where it would stay hidden until later, I smiled. Wouldn't it be amazing if I had purchased an actual miracle?

Chapter 3

THE CHUNNEL: A SPECIAL TRAIN THAT TRAVELS BENEATH THE ENGLISH CHANNEL, CONNECTING ENGLAND AND FRANCE

"I wish she'd take a gap year," I heard my dad say to my mum as I approached the front room. "What's the hurry anyway?"

Great, I thought. *More Alice and university talk. Just what we need.*

"Peter, we've been over this," Mum said. "Alice has said a gap year doesn't interest her. And if there isn't anything she'd love to be doing for a year before beginning university, then what's the point, really? Generally, kids who take gap years want to travel."

"Or they need to work to make money," Dad said. "Sometimes I wonder if we should press the issue a bit more with her."

"She'll get financial aid," Mum said. "Some scholarships, hopefully. And there are always loans. I just thought we'd have more money for the travel that will be necessary for flying her back and forth during holidays."

Alice had applied to a number of top schools in America, where she planned on studying pre-med. Her number-one choice was the University of Southern California. She wouldn't hear back for another month or so as to where she'd be going, but with her outstanding grades, there was no doubt she'd be getting in *somewhere*.

I was about to clear my throat, to let them know I was there, since I seemed to be invisible a lot of the time these days, but I didn't get a chance. Alice came barreling past me. "Is it too late for me to apply to Cornell?" she asked. "It's in New York." She groaned as she closed her eyes briefly, like she was in pain. "I can't believe I didn't apply to any schools in New York."

"Sweetheart, you really shouldn't choose a college

solely because of a boy you've known only briefly," Dad said.

"I'm not, Dad! It's a really good school."

"Is this going to take a while?" I asked with a sigh. "Because I'll go sit in my room and wait if it is."

"No," Dad said. "We're leaving now. Alice, we'll have to discuss this later; I'm sorry."

Dad gave Mum a quick kiss good-bye and then led us around back where the wagons are stored to transport items between the shop and home. It was a cool and cloudy morning, pretty typical April weather, as the three of us trudged down the sidewalk pulling our wagons of antiques. The Little Shop of Treasures isn't too far from where we live.

"I don't know why you're making us come with you," Alice said as we weaved around a steady stream of people coming out of a café. "You get along fine without us while we're in school."

"I can use all the help I can get today," Dad replied as he gave a wave to a man setting a sign outside his shop. "It's a lot of work cleaning up new pieces, adding them to the inventory, and tagging them before they're put on display."

He'd brought home two large bags of items, which we'd carried on to the Chunnel with us in Paris. *I'd* told him he should have shipped the stuff home, but *he'd* said he didn't want to wait for all of it to arrive. When Alice and I were younger, Dad took these trips on his own. We were always *so* excited to see what he brought home for us. It was almost as fun as Christmas, as he pulled items from his bag and handed them over.

One time, when he came home from a trip, he'd handed Alice a six-inch ceramic figurine of a girl with golden hair wearing a long, mint-green dress with white-and-gold accents and a matching hat, carrying a dainty little basket. I thought she was the most beautiful figurine I'd ever seen. When he handed me my gift, a vintage toy horse, I had to blink back the tears because I was so disappointed. I wanted that ceramic figurine he'd given Alice. Somehow I managed a polite thank-you. But Alice saw right through me.

"Dad?" she'd asked. "Is it all right if Phoebe and I trade? I think she'd rather have this figurine, and I'd much rather have the pretty horse."

Dad had simply shrugged and told us it was fine with him, if that's what we both wanted. I'd flung my little arms around Alice's neck and hugged her as I blinked back happy tears.

If that happened today, I thought, she'd probably ask if she could have both the figurine and the horse and leave me with nothing.

Now Alice prodded him in regard to the lot of antiques he'd brought home. "Are you disappointed you didn't find anything amazing?"

"I try to keep my expectations low," Dad replied, "but my optimism high. Which means I'm always hoping I might find something great, but I never really expect it. If that makes sense."

"Dad?" I asked.

"Yes?"

"Does it happen very often?"

"Does what happen very often?"

"You know, finding the painting or the vase worth a half a million pounds?"

He gave me a tiny little smile. "Not nearly often enough. But that's partly what makes those things so valuable."

I thought of the compact in my bag, and for a moment, I was tempted to share it with them. But I wanted to know more about the item first, if possible.

Besides, I liked having a secret that was all mine and no one else's. It made me feel important. Special. I hadn't felt that way much lately, what with my parents being so consumed with Alice's university stuff.

We walked in silence for a little while until Alice let out a heavy sigh. "Do you think Justin misses me as much as I miss him?"

"How am I supposed to know?" I replied. "Why don't you ring him and find out?"

"Because I don't want to be the annoying, needy girl. I emailed him as soon as we got home, but I haven't heard from him yet. Unfortunately, some people don't check their email very often. I need to wait for him to respond, as difficult as it might be."

Did she really believe that was the reason, or was she just telling herself that to make herself feel better? It seemed to me like if he missed her as much as she missed him, he would have replied immediately.

I stifled a yawn. "I think you need to try to take your mind off of Justin. How about you try to *not* talk about him for the next few hours? Or give us a real treat and try for all day."

She stopped in her tracks, her brown eyes glaring at me. "Phoebe, you are *so* mean."

I couldn't help but laugh. "That's twice today you've said that. Can't you see that I'm trying to help you?"

She took off in a huff, rushing past me, her brown ponytail bobbing about in such a way it reminded me of a squirrel's tail. "But you're not," she called back at me. "If you wanted to help me, you'd let me talk about him as much as I like."

"Fine, Alice. Talk about him and be miserable all day if that's what you want. See if I care."

She slowed down a bit, and I caught up to her. When I glanced over, I noticed she was biting her bottom lip, as if trying to keep back the tears. I quickly decided that if she started crying there, in the middle of the sidewalk for the world to see, I would cross the street and pretend I'd never seen her before.

"You don't understand," she said as we walked together again. "How could you? You're only twelve. I feel like I might have met the person who's meant to be my one true love, and now I may never see him again."

I couldn't let it go. I stopped and faced her. "Alice. True love? What a bunch of rubbish. You only knew him for three days!"

She looked like she wanted to tear into me, but Dad, who had been walking ahead of us the entire time, turned and glared at us. "Girls. Please. That's enough. It's just two more blocks and then we'll be at the shop. How about we keep our thoughts to ourselves for now? All right?"

"Fine," Alice said, her face hard and cold.

"Perfect," I said, because honestly, her love life was about the last thing I wanted to discuss.

Going to work with Dad used to be fun for us. If only she'd start acting like a regular person again. Someone I'd actually want to be around. Of course, Dad had said her behavior was all *completely* normal, but I just didn't see how that could be true. We'd always gotten along so well. And now . . . ugh. I could hardly stand to be around her for ten minutes.

The more I thought about it, the sadder I became. I wanted to fix things between us, but how? How could I do that when it seemed all we did was argue?

I vowed then and there to find a way. There had to be *something* I could do.

Chapter 4

STRAIGHT AWAY: IMMEDIATELY

When we stepped inside The Little Shop of Treasures, the familiar smell of musty old stuff combined with Mum's favorite floral air freshener made me smile. Even if I find shopping for antiques frustrating sometimes, I do love this cute little shop. For a while, Dad tried to keep things categorized—a section for dishes, another for clocks, one for figurines, etc. But eventually, as he acquired more and more pieces, the place kind of took on a life of its own, and now, there is no rhyme or reason to what goes where, and it's so much more fun that way.

There's lots of old furniture scattered about—chairs, hutches, bureaus, and tables. Jewelry is locked up in a glass case by the cash register, along with a large selection of coins and some old pocketknives. Pictures are hung on the walls.

He bought the business when I was six, so I was old enough to understand that the vintage toys he brought into the shop weren't to be played with. Still, they've always been my favorite things to look at—old cars and double-decker buses, dolls and action figures, wooden blocks and spinning tops. When I was eight, I fell in love with a really old stuffed little bear, and I couldn't stop talking about him. I named him Nicky, because he wore a pair of red knickers and I thought that was so funny. For Christmas that year, Dad wrapped Nicky up and gave him to me. I still have him in my room, on a shelf.

When we stepped through the front door, Dad flipped the sign in the front window so it read OPEN. Then he turned and stroked his mustache as he surveyed the place.

"Everything all right, Dad?" I asked.

"Yes. Just fine. Looks like Martin sold the cherry

curio last week while we were away. I wonder how much he fetched for it."

Martin is Dad's one part-time employee. He's in his sixties and he absolutely loves old things, as well as chit-chatting with people. Dad has said a number of times he doesn't know what he'd do without Martin. It's because of him that Dad is able to travel to Paris a couple of times a year to look for new antiques.

"Okay," Dad said, "let's get these wagons unloaded straight away."

We headed toward the inventory room at the back of the shop. There's a desk with a computer and a couple of tables and chairs, as well as a sink and cleaning supplies. While Dad cleared away some of the clutter, Alice and I began setting boxes onto the tables. Almost everything was in a box to keep the items as protected from damage as possible.

The bell above the door jingled, alerting us to a customer, so Dad hurried out. As soon as he was gone, Alice leaned against one of the tables and pulled out her phone.

"Hooray," she said, "Kiera's texted that she's back from holiday. I've missed her so much." She motioned toward the back door. "I'm going to step outside and give her a ring."

As soon as I was alone, I went to the computer and turned it on. While I waited for it to power up, I took the compact out of my pocket. I was so curious how much it might be worth. A hundred pounds? A thousand? Or maybe I was completely wrong about the whole thing, and it was only worth what I'd paid for it. I didn't think that could be true, but I was no expert, so anything was possible.

I peeked out the window to check on Alice. She was talking up a storm, her free hand waving around. Poor Kiera was probably getting an earful about Justin. Well, better her than me.

Returning my attention back to the compact, I opened it. Inside, there was a mirror on the top half, and on the bottom, a little tray for holding powered makeup and an applicator. But here, there was no makeup. Instead, there was a black-and-white photo of a girl who had chin-length dark hair with tight curls around the bottom half. She wore a sweater with a blazer over it, and to me, her face looked sad, since she wasn't smiling.

I'd seen the photo before, when I'd opened up the

case to see what was inside after I'd returned to our hotel in Paris. But it was only now that I noticed something underneath the photo—a neatly folded piece of stationery.

I heard footsteps coming my way, so I opened the top desk drawer and threw everything in it before I sat down in front of the computer.

"Where's Alice?" Dad asked when he stepped into the room.

I clicked on the inventory software icon to open it. "Outside. Talking to Kiera on her phone."

"You sure you don't mind her doing that? I mean, she'll be back to help you, right?"

"Once she tells Kiera all about her broken heart, yes, I'm sure she'll be back to help. Meanwhile, I quite like the peace and quiet."

Dad chuckled. "Okay, then. I'll be up front if you need me for anything."

I pretended to be concentrating on the computer program. "Mm-hm," is all I said.

After he left, I checked the window again. Alice could come in at any time, but for now, she seemed engrossed in conversation with her friend.

I dashed back to the desk drawer and pulled out the folded piece of paper. I'm pretty sure I didn't let out a single breath as I read the one-page letter written in cursive handwriting.

September 28, 1941

Dear Kitty,

I can't believe it's now been two years since we've seen you. Mama, Papa, and I, we miss you so. But as long as the war rages on, they believe you are better off staying with your evacuee host family there in the peaceful countryside. Enclosed is a picture of me, taken recently. I know you wanted to see me in my ARP uniform, but hopefully you will understand that I only want to wear that thing when I absolutely have to.

Don't laugh, but my friend Mary Jane has a great-grandmother who believes in magic and spells. I asked her for a spell that might bring two people together when there is distance between them. She gave me this list of activities I must do, telling me it works for distance between two people in more ways than one. Kitty, please believe me when I tell you I'm trying to do everything on it so we can once again be together as the loving sisters we once were. Cross your fingers it works!

30

Find the boy who will always be a boy and circle it three times.

Leave an invisible handprint at the place where opera singers once performed before a fire changed everything.

There are four corners of the square, but only three are occupied. Visit the empty space, place a coin, and make a wish.

Close your eyes and hold your breath as you walk through the door of this church with a crypt, beneath a clock and a steeple.

Blow a kiss through the window of the Indian restaurant where Winston Churchill once dined.

Wave to the songbirds and woodpeckers who come here to visit the dead while taking in the spectacular view.

A lion waits for you above a tea shop. Leave him a gift in the hollow pillar.

Your loving sister,
Sheila

Chapter 5

MARMITE: A THICK, STICKY BROWN SAVORY SPREAD

The makeup compact I'd bought that might be worth a nice amount of money was suddenly *so* much more.

A letter over seventy years old?

A girl living with an evacuee host family?

An ARP uniform?

A spell to bring two people together?

It was all a bit strange but also *really* amazing. Alice had done a big project on the Blitz a few years back, and she'd asked me to help glue photos on a poster board for her. Before helping her, I'd known that the Blitz was when Nazi Germany bombed us for almost a year during World

War II. Everyone in London grows up knowing about the Blitz. But I remember learning some things I hadn't known before. Like, I hadn't realized that in an effort to keep millions of children safe, they were sent away to live in the countryside or even to other countries.

It was almost hard to imagine, but I could tell from Sheila's letter that her sister Kitty was one of those children.

I desperately wanted to read the letter again, more slowly this time, but since Alice could walk in at any moment, I decided the best thing to do was to shove the entire lot back into my coat pocket, where it remained for the rest of the day. Alice came back inside shortly after I read the letter, so I'd done the right thing.

While I typed the new stuff into the program on the computer, I managed to sneak in a search for a Cartier makeup compact, but nothing came up. That told me we'd never had one like it in the store. I wasn't sure where else to look to figure out its value. Dad had books and certain online sites he used, but I didn't really know about any of that.

Still, while I might not have known how much the compact was worth, I was determined to find out more about that strange letter and what it all meant. For lunch we had Marmite sandwiches that Mum had made (no cooking required, thankfully) and while we ate, I decided to pick Dad's brain a bit.

"Dad?"

"Yes?"

"When the children got sent away, before the Blitz, did they have to go all by themselves?"

He stopped chewing and set his sandwich down. "That's a rather odd question to ask, Phoebe. What made you think of it?"

I hadn't expected him to question me about *my* question. I had to think fast. "Oh, well, when we were traveling home on the Chunnel, I heard an old woman saying something about living with an evacuee host family when she was a child. And it just got me thinking about it. I meant to ask you earlier, and then I forgot. I'm simply curious about it, that's all."

This answer seemed to satisfy him, as he nodded his head and leaned back in his chair, stroking his mustache a bit. "I see. Well, yes, Operation Pied Piper was the project's name, and you're correct—if children were old enough, they were sent away without their parents. Some teachers went along, however, as supervisors."

"How old were the children?" I asked, as I wondered how old Kitty might have been.

"I'm not sure exactly," he replied. "I'm guessing from the very young, who went with their mothers, all the way up to fourteen or fifteen. At a certain age, the older children, as teenagers, could go to work to help the war effort."

"Is that what the ARP was?" I asked, hoping he wouldn't think this was an even stranger question than my first one. "Something to help with the war effort?"

He nodded as he wiped his mouth. "Yes. ARP stands for Air Raid Precautions. They handed out gas masks and helped deliver messages during the air raids, among other things. I'm glad you're interested in history, Phoebe. Perhaps you should check out some books from the library. They would probably be more reliable than my awful memory."

"Good idea," I said. "Maybe I'll do that." I had one more question I wanted to ask him, though. "Do you think there are many people still alive who were children during the war?"

"Of course there are," Alice said as she stood up to throw her trash away. "You said yourself you heard a woman talking about it. There are lots of eighty-year-olds walking around, aren't there? Quite a few of them even come into this shop."

It made me wonder—could Sheila or Kitty still be alive? If so, might they be here, in London, even? I'd found the compact in Paris, so perhaps Kitty had ended up there eventually. It was anyone's guess, really, since a lot can happen in seventy years. But without a last name, it seemed like trying to find one or both of them would be about as easy as finding a single marble in a giant gumball machine.

Just then, the jingle of the bell alerted us to a customer. My dad started to get up, until we heard, "It's only me, Mr. Ainsworth. That annoying chap who's always wanting a look at your old pocketknives."

The three of us glanced at one another and smiled. "Back here, Ned," Dad called out.

Ned is the grandson of Mr. and Mrs. Halliday, who own the bookshop nearby. He and I met shortly after Dad bought the antiques shop, since we're the same age, and because he's so happy and silly all the time, I liked him immediately. We've been friends ever since. He likes to look at the pocketknives because he's active in Scouts, and loves stuff like hiking and camping, which I don't understand at all. Sleeping on the ground, in the woods, with insects and wild animals, doesn't sound fun to me. It sounds . . . awful!

He stuck his tall, lanky self through the door and said, "You're having lunch and didn't invite me?"

"Want my crusts?" I asked him, holding one out.

He walked over and grabbed it out of my hand and stuck it in his mouth. "Thanks," he mumbled as he chewed. When he'd finished he said, "Nana only brought one sandwich for me today. Guess we didn't have enough bread for more." He jingled some change in his pocket. "Shall we walk up to the sweet shop, Pheebs? My treat."

I hopped up. "Yes, please. I've been in this stuffy old shop all morning. It's all right, isn't it, Dad? We won't be gone too long."

"I suppose you do deserve a break," he said.

I pulled on Ned's sleeve. "Come on, then. Before he changes his mind and puts us both to work."

He waved to my dad and Alice before we ducked out the back door. "Thank you for saving me," I said as we walked around the row of buildings to get the sidewalk.

"What did I save you from, exactly?" he asked.

"Work, mostly, but my lovesick sister as well. She seems to be a person I don't even know anymore."

He ducked to avoid a low tree branch as he looked at me quizzically. "Lovesick? Didn't know she was seeing anyone."

"She met him in Paris. Justin, from America. Only spent a few hours with him, really, but she's sure she's now lost her one true love. But let's not talk about that. I want to tell you about what I found in Paris."

"Let me guess. A vintage pogo stick?"

I couldn't help but smile. "No."

"A cat that weighs forty-three kilos?"

"You are so cheeky. Not even close."

"A cat that weights a hundred and nineteen kilos?"

I laughed. "Wrong again."

"All right. I guess you'll just have to tell me." We reached the front door of the Sweet Palace. "After we choose our sweets, of course."

Ned got his usual, licorice torpedos, while I chose some pear drops. As we strolled along outside, munching on our goodies, I told him that inside one of the antiques we brought back from Paris, I'd found an old photo and a letter. I decided to keep the information about the compact to myself, until I learned more about it. I didn't want to look like an idiot if it turned out to be nothing.

I summarized Sheila's letter to Kitty as best I could from memory. Ned didn't say a single word the entire time, which was unusual for him. He always seemed to have something to say. When I finished, I asked, "So. What do you think?"

He scratched his head, which was covered with a mop of sandy blond hair, and said, "I think that's incredible, Pheebs. I really do. It makes you wonder if that magic spell, or whatever it was, worked, and if Kitty got to come home soon after that."

"I know. I'm so curious about what happened to her. To both of them, really." We both stopped in front of Halliday's, the bookshop Ned's grandparents own. The front window was decorated with toy trains, planes, and automobiles, and there were books for both kids and adults featuring travel in some way. *The Hobbit* by J.R.R. Tolkien was front and center, reminding me how much I wanted to read it.

I opened the front door and poked my head in. His grandmother was at the counter, reading a magazine. "Hello, Mrs. Halliday," I said with a wave.

"Hello, Phoebe. Nice to see you. Working with your dad today?"

"Yes. We brought lots of stuff home from Paris. Have a good afternoon!"

"You too," she said before I closed the door.

Ned popped another sweet into his mouth. "Phoebe, I think you should have your sister do the spell. She could see if it might work to bring her and the bloke from America back together again."

When he said that, I almost choked on my pear drop. It hadn't even occurred to me that the spell could work today. "Do you think that's possible? To do the activities in the letter now, all these years later?"

He shrugged. "It would be fun to try, wouldn't it? Why, are you going to tell Alice about what you've found?"

I shook my head. "No. I'm not going to tell anyone, except you, because *I* want to visit the places in the spell."

"What? Why?" Ned asked, clearly confused. "Who do you want to bring closer to you?"

"My sister!"

Now Ned laughed. "But she *lives* with you. You can't get much closer than that, can you?"

"Not closer physically," I explained. "The letter says 'it works for distance between two people in more ways than one.' Alice and I used to be really close. Like friends, you know? Now we can hardly stand each other. And I want to fix that before she goes all the way to America." I grabbed his arm. "Ned, will you go with me? Around London, and help me find each place on the list? You love a fun adventure, don't you?"

He took another torpedo and popped it in his mouth. "That I do."

"Good. Then you'll do it?" I clasped my hands together out in front of me. "Please?"

"All right. If you'll do something for me in return."

I eyed him suspiciously. "What would that be?"

"Mum's fortieth birthday is on Friday, and we're having a big party for her. We sent an invitation over last week, while you were in Paris. Did your mum say anything to you about it?"

"No. She must have forgotten to tell us. I'll ask her about it when we get home. Do you need help with the party, then?"

"No, that's not it. You see, I haven't a clue what to get her for a gift. While we're out and about, will you help me find something?"

"Ned, you're such a good artist. Why don't you draw her a picture?"

He sighed. "Because I've done that before. Many times, actually. This year, I want to get her something really special. So please, will you help me?"

I held my hand out. "All right. It's a deal."

As he shook my hand, he said, "She might like a vintage pogo stick. Do you happen to have one of those in the shop?"

"Afraid not, Ned. Besides, I really don't see your mum getting up on one of those things and hopping down the street."

"How about a nice, extremely fat cat? I'm not picky."

I reached into my bag of sweets and threw one of my pear drops at him, which he skillfully caught with his hand. He then popped it into his mouth and said, "Throw me another, would you? That's delicious."

So I did, which he caught again. "I've quite missed you, Ned Chapman."

"You only like me because I buy you sweets."

"You're exactly right about that," I said with a grin.

Chapter 6

THE TUBE: **LONDON'S PUBLIC UNDERGROUND**

TRANSIT SYSTEM

I want to send Justin something special in the mail," Alice said as we set the table for supper. "Any ideas, Mum?"

Once again, I seemed to be invisible. I was getting used to the feeling, and yet, I still didn't like it. It's like getting up early for school every day. The alarm goes off Monday through Friday and it's not a surprise, but I would be much happier if it didn't go off at all.

"Hm," Mum replied. "Do you mean a gift of some kind?"

"Sort of," Alice said. "Something that lets him know I'm thinking of him."

"What about a framed photo of the two of you?" I suggested. "You took some while you were in Paris, didn't you?"

Alice tucked the last cloth napkin next to a plate before she looked at me. "Phoebe, that's actually a brilliant idea."

She sounded so surprised that instead of feeling happy, I felt a bit insulted. Like she didn't think I was capable of any good ideas.

"Well, thanks," I said quietly as I placed the silverware next to each plate. "I think."

"I need to select the best one and print it out. Then tomorrow I'll go shopping for a frame. Sound good, Mum?"

"Fine with me," she said.

Alice plunked herself down in a chair and started scrolling through the photos on her phone.

"Let's go finish the salad," Mum said to me.

When we reached the kitchen counter, I told her, "I wanted to ask you something."

"Sure," she replied.

"I saw Ned today, and he wanted to know if I might take the Tube into the city with him tomorrow. Would that be all right?"

She went to work slicing up the cucumber. "What for?"

"His mum's birthday is coming up. He said they invited us to her party. On Friday, I believe. Did you get the invitation?"

She smiled. "Oh, yes. That's right. I did get it. I forgot to mention it to you."

"We're going to go, aren't we?" I asked while I grabbed the container of sesame seeds.

"Of course. Sounds like fun. So he wants your help with some shopping?"

"Yes. He's not sure what to get her for a gift, so I told him I'd be happy to help him."

It wasn't exactly a lie. But it wasn't the entire truth, either. Still, I didn't want to tell her about the magic spell that Sheila had mentioned. I wasn't sure what Mum would have said about it, and the last thing I needed was for her to tell me I couldn't go.

"You can't go shopping around here?" she asked as she dropped the cucumber slices into the salad bowl full of lettuce.

"Well, he doesn't *want* to go shopping here. What's the problem?"

Mum sighed. "I don't know. I worry, I guess. The two of you, in the big city, by yourselves."

"We'll be fine," I told her. "We've been on the Tube hundreds of times."

"Yes, but not by yourselves," she said. Then her eyes got big. "I don't have to work tomorrow, so I could go with you. What about that? I could treat you to a nice luncheon. Doesn't that sound lovely?"

I gulped. Having my mother go along with us would certainly *not* be lovely.

"What are you two discussing?" Alice asked as she walked in and grabbed a piece of bread from the breadbasket.

"I want to go into London tomorrow with Ned, and Mum doesn't trust us to go alone," I said.

"Sweetheart," she said, her bottom lip sticking out a tiny bit, like I'd hurt her feelings. "It's not that I don't trust you."

"Then please, let us go."

Mum turned to Alice. "Perhaps you could go with them?" She looked at me. "Would that be better than me tagging along?"

Alice didn't give me a chance to respond. "Um, no. I'm not going to do that. I spent enough time with her in Paris. Let her and Ned go, if that's what she wants. You can't baby her forever."

Part of me wanted to hug my sister and the other part wanted to slug her in the arm. *I spent enough time with her Paris?* The way she said it, she made it sound like every minute spent in my presence was like a minute spent in misery. Like spending time with me was as bad as sitting in a jail cell with only bread and water for nourishment.

I shook my head, wondering once again how we'd gotten here, to this place where things were so difficult between us. It was just one more reason why I had to do the things in the letter, and see if the spell could work its magic on the two of us.

As much as I might have liked to make her feel bad about that comment, I decided to ignore it. "I can check in with you throughout the day," I told my mother. "Text you every couple of hours. If that'll make you feel better?"

It took a moment, but she finally nodded. "All right. You can go. But please, be careful, all right?"

I walked over and gave her a quick hug. "You know we will be."

"When's supper going to be ready?" Alice asked as she finished off her piece of bread. "I'm starving."

Mum looked at me, since I'd been the one to put the chicken in the oven for roasting. "About ten more minutes," I replied. "I'm going to grate a carrot for the salad. Mum, can you chop up a tomato?"

"You got it," she said. She looked at my sister. "Did you find a good photo of the two of you?"

"I think so. I wish I'd taken more. Too late now, though."

"Would you like me to go shopping with you?" Mum asked. "To find a frame?"

"No," she said. "I can do it on my own. I'll go in the morning. Then I'll write him a nice letter to go with it."

"Alice?" Mum said. She was chopping the tomato slowly, like she was thinking very hard about what she was going to say next.

"Yeah?"

"I think perhaps you should prepare yourself for the worst."

"What do you mean?" she asked, her forehead all wrinkled with worry.

"I mean, it's possible Justin isn't interested in a long-distance relationship. They're not exactly easy, especially when you're as young as the two of you."

"That's why I need to apply to a school in New York," Alice said.

"But where's Justin going to university?" I asked.

"He's a year younger than me," Alice replied. "So he still has a whole year in New York."

With the meat thermometer in hand, I opened the oven door. After I got a reading on the chicken, I said, "It's ready."

"Alice, will you go let your father know?" Mum asked. "He's in his study."

I could only hope we'd find something else to talk about around the dining table. If only there was some magical spell to get my sister to stop thinking about a certain boy!

After we ate, I went to my room and texted Ned the details about where and when to meet the next day. I was so excited to find out if the spell actually worked! I picked up a pink notecard so I could write something to go on my happiness board. Since my parents might see it, I couldn't write anything about the compact or the letter. So I wrote this:

Ned and I are going shopping in London tomorrow!

As I pinned the card to my bulletin board, I smiled. It was going to be a wonderful adventure, and I could hardly wait.

Chapter 7

CRUMBLE: BAKED FRUIT TOPPED WITH A CRUMBLY

MIXTURE OF FLOUR, SUGAR, AND BUTTER

Good morning, Pheebs," Ned said when we met at the Tube station the next day. It was gray and chilly out, but no rain, thankfully.

"Hello," I said as I stared at something round in his hand. "What have you got there?"

"A compass."

"Oh." I smiled. "Are you worried we might get lost? Because I have my phone, complete with GPS and everything."

"But we can't use your phone," he told me, looking quite serious as he said it.

"We can't? Why not?"

"Because this is supposed to be a fun adventure. That's what you told me it would be. Remember?"

I gave him a nod. "Yes. I remember. I still don't understand, though."

"It won't be much fun if we look everything up so it's all too easy. The girl who wrote the letter you found. What's her name?"

"Sheila."

"Right. Did Sheila have a phone to help her out?"

"No, silly. It was 1941. They didn't have cell phones then."

He stuck out his chest triumphantly. "Exactly. She would be so disappointed in us if we made it easy on ourselves."

I thought of Nora and myself, and how we'd navigated Paris and her grandmother's treasure hunt simply by reading the notes she'd left and talking to the people she'd mentioned. It'd been fun, meeting new people and hearing stories about Grandma Sylvia. Sure, Nora had been nervous at first, since she's much more shy than I am. But as we went along, it got easier for her. The longer I thought about it, the more I liked Ned's idea.

The train came just then, so I waited to say anything else. Ned stepped ahead and I followed after him. Once we sat down, I said, "I agree. We shouldn't use our phones. But how is a compass going to help us?"

He shrugged. "I figure we might get lost."

"But Ned, I'm pretty sure a compass only helps if you're lost in the *woods*. If we get lost in London, we simply need to ask someone. They'll be happy to help us."

He stared at me for a moment. Then he shoved the compass into the pocket of his jacket. "Good point. I hadn't thought of that."

I gave him a little shove. "You're so funny." Then I pointed to the map on the wall. "Do you know which stop we get off at? For the Peter Pan statue?"

"Are you sure that's the right place?"

"Positive," I said as I pulled the letter out of my bag. "Here's the clue: *Find the boy who will always be a boy and circle it three times*. It has to be Peter Pan. Who else could it be?"

He considered the question for a moment before he finally said, "Phoebe, are you always right about everything?"

"No. If I'm your sister, I'm usually wrong about everything."

"Good thing you're not my sister."

I studied the letter. "The first and last ones are easy. It's the ones in between that are going to be hard to figure out."

Ned tapped the letter with his finger. "But if Sheila figured it out, so can we."

"Thanks again for doing this with me," I said. "It's much more fun than doing it by myself."

"Not a problem. I didn't have anything planned anyhow. Chester's away on holiday."

Chester is Ned's best friend. I've met him a couple of times. He's pretty shy. Nothing like Ned, basically.

"What do you guys like to do for fun?" I asked.

"Besides camp and stuff like that?"

"Yeah, besides that."

"You'll laugh."

"I promise I won't."

"You will."

"Ned. We've been friends for a long time. I would never be mean to you. Or at least, not on purpose, anyway."

He sighed and looked out the window for a moment. Then he turned to me and said, "Fine. We like to bake. Crumbles and pies. That kind of thing."

I smiled. "I love that."

"You're teasing."

"No. I'm not. I really think it's great. I like to cook, too, remember?"

"But you cook real food. Meals and stuff. We don't do any of that. Just desserts for us."

"Dessert is real food. What's the best thing you two have made?"

"We made a delicious plum crumble a few months ago. Ate the whole thing, the two of us. Mum asked me what had happened to it, and when I told her we ate it all, she nearly fell over."

"Didn't you feel sick after eating it all?"

He grinned. "No. It was so delicious, Pheebs. Does that sound like I'm bragging?"

"Not to me, it doesn't. But now I'm hungry for some crumble."

"Me too," he replied. "Will we have time to get something to eat while we're in the city?"

"Does Peter Pan fly?"

"Is that a yes?"

"That's a yes," I said.

"Good. This day just keeps getting better and better."

I could only hope that would continue.

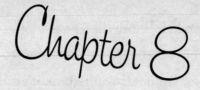

Chapter 8

BISCUITS: COOKIES

The Peter Pan statue is located in Kensington Gardens, next to Hyde Park. When we got off the Tube at Lancaster Gate, we made our way in the right direction.

"It's past the Italian Gardens," Ned said as we walked.

"I know," I replied. "Past the drinking fountain with the two bears hugging each other at the top of it."

"Grandpa told me that fountain was once used by cattle and horses. Right as I was about to stick my face in there." He shuddered. "I turned around and yelled, 'And you're letting me *drink* from it? Ew!' He thought that was so funny."

56

"At least he didn't tell you after you'd gotten a drink."

"You're right. That would have been far worse."

We walked past Long Water, a lake that runs through the middle of the gardens. Ducks paddled around in the water and birds perched on the wooden posts. I thought of Sheila, coming here all of those years ago, hoping to create a bit of magic that would bring her sister home. Did she come alone, I wondered, or did she ask a friend to come along with her, like I did? Maybe Mary Jane went with her to keep her company. I found myself hoping she did. Thinking of her wandering around London all by her lonesome made me a little sad for some reason.

Just then, my phone rang. I scrambled to pull it out of the side pocket of my bag and looked at the number. "My sister," I explained to Ned before answering.

"Hello?" I said.

"Phoebe?"

"That's me."

"Do you have Nora and Justin's address?"

"Yes. I have it. But so do you, right?"

She sniffled. "I can't find it. I think the piece of paper with his information might have accidentally been thrown out. I'm not sure, but I've looked everywhere, and it's just . . . gone."

"Hm. Sorry."

"I'm not calling for your sympathy. I need their address. I want to get this package mailed off to him today."

Ned stopped walking and looked at me, probably concerned since I had apologized. Like maybe something terrible happened. But no, nothing terrible had happened at all, it was just my sister, being her usual demanding self.

I rolled my eyes. "Maybe you should text Justin and ask him for it."

"I can't," she whined. "I want it to be a surprise."

"I don't have it with me, Alice. It's in my room somewhere. I'll look for it when I get home."

"Phoebe," she cried. "I don't want to get it when you get home. I want it *now*."

I stared out at the water, wondering why every little thing between us had to turn into a battle. "But I'm not home right now, am I? I'm in London, with Ned. And I don't want you tearing my room apart. So you'll just have to wait. See you later today. Bye."

"No, don't—"

I didn't want to wait to see what she was going to say. Because I could pretty much guess what it would be. She'd tell me I was being ridiculous and that all I needed to do was to tell her where the address was so she could get it. Except I didn't want her poking her nose around in my room and my stuff.

"Everything all right?" Ned asked.

I stuffed my phone back in my bag and started walking again. "I told you she's being impossible these days. The only time she'll voluntarily talk to me is when she wants something. The rest of the time, I'm basically invisible."

"What do you mean by that?" Ned asked as he walked beside me. "Invisible?"

Ned was an only child. It made sense that he'd probably never felt that way.

"I'm not sure I can explain it very well, but I'll try. You know how the earth revolves around the sun? Well, in our house, lately everything revolves around Alice. I feel like a dinky little star in the night sky that no one notices. And to be honest, sometimes I find myself wondering if I even have a place in the galaxy at all."

I looked over at Ned and he had a scowl on his face. "Phoebe, that is a terribly sad thing to say. Of course you have a place in the galaxy. *Everyone* has a place in the galaxy. You need to claim your place and be the shining star you are, no matter what anyone else is doing."

I closed one eye and looked at Ned with suspicion. "Are you secretly a poet or something?"

He chuckled. "I wish. But poet or not, I mean it."

"The problem is, I can never outshine the sun," I said.

"Maybe not," he replied, "but who cares? Not me. And I bet your parents are glad they don't have two suns. That would be really hot. And annoying. Can you imagine how much they'd sweat? It'd get quite stinky in your house, Pheebs."

It made me laugh.

"They all love you, you know," he said. "Even if it doesn't feel like it all the time."

"I know," I said. "Still, it would be nice if my sister and I could at least get along. Whether we're a star and a sun or a sister and a sister. That's why this spell has to work."

When we reached the statue, a woman was taking photos of two little girls standing on either side of it. One of the girls was tall and skinny, about seven or eight, with her blonde hair brushed back into a ponytail. The other one was short and stocky, age four or five, with curly brown hair and a smile so bright, I wanted to scoop her up and give her a squeeze.

"Splendid," the woman said. "Let's do one more. How about you look up at Peter and give him a little wave?"

The girls did as she said and when the woman was finished taking the picture, she turned and looked at us. "Thank you for your patience. It's all yours. If you wanted a photo, I mean."

"Are they your daughters?" I asked.

"They are indeed," she said as she watched the girls chase each other around the statue, their giggles sweeter than a pear drop.

It made my heart happy and sad all at the same time. Sad because that used to be my sister and me. Joined at the hip—that's what my father used to say about us. Where one girl was, the other one wanted to be. Always.

"Do they get along like that all of the time?" I asked.

The woman laughed as she tucked her phone into her bag and slung it over her shoulder. "Oh, heavens no. Not at all. The youngest can be quite the pill at times, and the older one loses her temper easily. It gets . . . interesting. But that's what sisters do, I suppose, and so I wouldn't change a thing."

"You wouldn't?" I asked just as the younger one pulled the older girl's ponytail, causing her to cry out in pain. The older one spun around and grabbed her sister's arm and yanked on it. The little one stood there for a brief second before she squeezed her eyes shut, clenched her fists, and burst into tears.

"Oh dear," their mum said, rushing over. "Trixie, you can't pull your sister's hair like that. You know it's not nice, and it never ends well."

The woman scooped Trixie up into her arms. The girl wrapped her small hands around her mother's neck and buried her face into her shoulder.

"Come along," she said as she held her hand out so the older girl could grab on to it. "Let's find a spot to sit in the gardens to enjoy our biscuits. Leave these two to enjoy Peter Pan in peace and quiet."

"Thank you!" Ned called out.

"You're welcome," the oldest girl called back, waving at us with her free hand.

"You better hurry," Ned told me. "Before some other people come."

I handed him my bag. "Do you think I should say anything?"

He gave me a quizzical look. "Like what?"

"I don't know. It seems a bit odd to just start going in circles."

Ned chuckled. "It's a magic spell, Pheebs. It *is* odd."

I turned around and looked behind me. A family of five was fast approaching. "Okay," I said. "Here I go."

I pretended to admire the statue in a big way as I walked around it once, twice, and finally three times. When I finished, I stepped back over to where Ned stood.

"I guess that's it," I told him. I nodded my head toward the family that now stood by the statue. "I think I'll ask them if they have any idea about the next place on the list. They seem nice enough, don't you think?"

"Great idea," he said.

It seemed to me this was another instance when the sweet angel face my sister had taught me to use when bartering might come in handy. So I put on my best friendly face and sweet innocent smile as I approached them before I said, "Excuse me?"

They turned. "Yes?" said the man.

"I was wondering, do you know London very well?" I asked.

"I'd say we do," the woman replied. "Why? Can we help you with something?"

I didn't want to show them the letter, because then I'd have to explain everything to them. So I simply asked, "Do you know of a place where opera singers once performed, before a fire changed everything?"

The man looked at his wife. "What's the music hall called between Wapping and Whitechapel? Near the Tower of London?"

"Wilton's," the woman replied as she watched her children, who had begun to play an imaginary game of Peter Pan. A boy pretending to be Peter flapped his arms and then stopped as the other two children, a girl and an older boy, came over to him.

"I'll be Tinkerbell," the little girl said.

"And I'll be Captain Hook," the boy said. "Which means I catch Tinkerbell and hide her from you." He grabbed his little sister. "Ahoy, matey, come and get her if ye dare."

"So you think that's the one, then?" I asked. "Opera singers definitely performed at Wilton's?"

"I'm not exactly sure of the history, to be honest," the woman said, "but it's been around a long, long time, and if I remember correctly, it's one of the few still standing that survived fire and flooding. Not to mention the Blitz."

The man nodded. "I'm almost positive it's the one you're looking for. Do you know how to get there from here?"

"I don't think we do, no."

The woman stepped away to keep the game of pretend from getting too rough while the man gave me directions. I scribbled them down using a pen and a small notebook from my bag.

"Thank you very much," I said.

"You're welcome," he replied.

And with that, the first item in the spell was done. I tried to see if I felt magical at all, but the only thing I felt was chilly. The sun still hadn't come out yet.

You can't rush magic, I guess.

Chapter 9

BROOD: A FAMILY OF YOUNG ANIMALS

I love England in the spring, with its pink camellias and yellow daffodils. And as I looked around while we strolled back toward the Tube station, I remembered one spring a number of years back when my family went to Green Park for a picnic on a pretty, sunny day. Green Park is one of the most famous parks for daffodils, and we managed to go on a day when everything was in full bloom. It was gorgeous. Alice had said, "Let's pretend we're fairies and we live here surrounded by daffodils."

"What do fairies eat?" I asked.

"I think they must eat anything that's sweet," Alice replied. "Maybe they make little tiny cakes out of dandelions and daisies."

"Oooh, I want a dandelion cake!" I exclaimed. "With lemon frosting."

And so, after we ate the lunch Mum had packed in a picnic basket, we made pretend dandelion cakes and played silly fairy games. Except at the time, they weren't silly at all, they were wonderful.

Sometimes I wonder if Alice ever remembers those times when we played and laughed and enjoyed each other's company. Maybe I should leave one of the family photo albums on her pillow, so she might flip through and be reminded that she didn't always find me as wonderful as a nest of wasps.

"Ned?"

"Yes?"

"Do you ever wish you had a brother or a sister?"

"All the time," he replied, looking across Long Water. "But Mum and Dad said I was enough for them."

"That makes it sound like you were quite a handful when you were a wee little lad."

He smiled. "I believe I was. According to them, from

the moment I woke up to the time I went to bed, I wanted to go, go, and go some more. You know my mother. She enjoys knitting. Reading. Quiet things. And I was not a very quiet little boy."

"Your grandparents own a bookshop," I said as stopped to look out at the water one last time before we left the gardens. A mother with a brood of ducklings was swimming toward the shore. "I bet you had to learn to be quiet, whether you wanted to be or not."

"You should hear my grandpa read out loud. He does the best voices. I was always entertained when I went there."

"And now when you visit, they put you to work."

"I like it, though. I like seeing what new books are coming in for the kid's section, especially. If there's something I want, they usually let me have it."

"I love that you have a library in your house. All those books shelved on the pretty bookshelves. It's really wonderful." Just then, an idea occurred to me. "Hey, maybe you should get your mother a nice, new book. If she likes to knit, you could get her a fun knitting book and some new yarn."

Ned made a funny face. "Phoebe, I wouldn't know the first thing about choosing yarn."

"Just get her favorite color or something. It can't be that hard."

He turned and started walking again. "You wouldn't think so, but I've been to the yarn shop and there are a gazillion kinds of yarn."

"A gazillion?" I asked with a smile. "I think you might be exaggerating."

"Maybe so. Anyway, she buys yarn all the time. I want to get her something unique. Something she'd never buy for herself, you know?"

"Ned, you do realize whatever you end up with, she's going to love it because *you* gave it to her."

"She wouldn't like a box of dirty socks."

"Well, no one would like that."

"Or, if I'm being completely honest, a pogo stick."

"Ha! I knew it! But I think you might be obsessed with pogo sticks."

"I'll admit it. I want one. They look like fun."

"Hey, what about a toy from the antique shop?" I asked. "Maybe you could find something from when she was a child."

"My mum isn't *that* old, Pheebs. Pretty sure the stuff in your store is from when my grandparents were young. Or even before that."

"I'm simply trying to help," I said.

"I know. I'm sure you'll think of something good. Eventually."

And here I thought completing all of the things in the letter was going to be the hard part.

Chapter 10

CRIKEY: AN EXCLAMATION OF SURPRISE

London is quite large. Much bigger than Paris, that's for sure. It seems people who don't know London very well are often surprised by this fact. Perhaps the idea of a palace and a royal family makes it seem like the setting for a cozy fairy tale. But *cozy* is not the word I would use to describe London. More like *sprawling*.

Although, when William and Kate got married, it did seem cozy for a moment. It was a day I'll never forget. Dad and Mum decided we shouldn't miss being a part of this important piece of history, so we woke up at five in the morning in order to get a good spot in

Parliament Square. We had a great view of the wedding party coming down the street in their horse-drawn carriages toward Westminster Abbey. Most of the onlookers wore red, white, and blue and waved flags in the air, proud to be British on the special day. You should have heard Alice waffle on after William and Kate appeared on the balcony and carried out the traditional kiss. The most romantic thing she'd ever seen, she'd said. "So lovely, so heartfelt, so . . ."

I couldn't let her continue. "Alice, it lasted about two seconds. Maybe less. It was a show for the crowd, that's all."

"You're such a little kid, you know that?" my sister had replied. "Just wait. Someday when you're older, you'll watch the film footage again and you'll see what I mean."

"Can we go home now?" I'd asked. I was tired. It had been a very long day.

The nice thing about London, though, is that the Tube makes it easy to get around the big city. It took Ned and I about thirty minutes to get from Kensington Gardens to the borough of Tower Hamlets, where the music hall is located. Once we made it to the small back street, however, things were not at all as we expected them to be. The street was blocked off because of construction.

"Oh no," I said, just as an elderly gentleman with a cane walked by us.

The man stopped and turned. "They've been working on repairs to Wilton's for a while now. It was desperately needed, you see. Wasn't stable at all. In fact, it was so bad in some rooms, the walls were actually crumbling."

"But we need to get over there," I said, a hint of desperation in my voice. "It's important."

"No. You mustn't," the old man replied. "It isn't safe. For anyone, but especially for children such as yourselves."

"All right," Ned said. "Thanks for letting us know."

The old man eyed us for a moment, probably not sure whether he could trust us to stay put, before he continued on his walk.

"We can't let a little construction get in our way," I told Ned.

"Maybe we should do some of the other things on the list and come back in a couple of days," Ned suggested. "They might open the street by then."

"But I can't do that."

"Why not?"

"Because I think I have to do the things in the order they're listed."

Ned crossed his arms over his chest and let out a small sigh. "Well, you don't know that for *sure*."

"No, but I can't risk ruining everything, either. So we have to do each item in the order it's listed. That's all there is to it."

We stood there and watched a couple of construction workers with hard hats and yellow coats talk to each other. One of them held a clipboard and glanced down at it every now and then.

"Maybe you can distract them while I run around the barricade and over to the door where I'll leave my handprint," I said.

"Distract them?" he asked. "And how, exactly, do you propose I do that?"

I nervously tugged at the sleeve of my jacket. "I don't know. You're a Scout. Get creative. That's what you'd do if you were lost in the woods, right?"

He reached into his pocket and pulled out his compass. "No, I'd use this."

"There has to be something you can do to get their attention for a minute," I said, looking around, as if the answer might suddenly appear.

"I could pretend to have a heart attack," he said.

I gave him a stern look. "Ned. You're only thirteen years old."

"We could buy some sweets, and I could pretend to choke."

"Um, do you really want them to whisk you away in an ambulance?" I replied. "Because that would not be funny at all."

He thought for a moment before he said, "What if I call them over and ask for directions? Pretend I don't have a phone or a compass in my pocket and it's very important I get somewhere or else I'm in big trouble."

I nodded. "That might work. Pick someplace far away and complicated to get to. While they're giving you directions, I'll slip away."

Ned approached the barricade and I followed. "Hello?" Ned called out. The two men looked over at us. "Could I bother you for a second?"

One of the men started walking toward us. The other one stayed put.

"Oh no," I whispered under my breath. The plan wouldn't work if both of them didn't come over to talk to Ned.

"What do you need?" the man asked.

"Directions. It's urgent. Can you help?" Ned paused. "It might take the both of you to figure it out."

I held my breath as I waited to see if both men would join us. When the other guy started walking, I slowly exhaled. Now I could only hope Ned had thought this out and had a good place in mind.

When both men were on the other side of the yellow plastic barricades, Ned told them, "I need to get to a bookshop. Halliday's. We're supposed to meet our mum there. Have you heard of it?"

Brilliant, I thought. Ned was asking directions to his grandparents' bookshop.

"Why don't you ring your mum and ask her?" the taller man asked.

"Don't have a phone," Ned replied.

"She lets you wander around London without a phone?" the shorter man said. "Crikey, that's not good. Is she daft?"

Hopefully, the phone in his pocket wouldn't suddenly start ringing. Wouldn't that make things interesting? And quite difficult? The funny thing was that Ned seemed to take offense to the man's comments, even though the story was entirely made up. "She's not daft, just poor. Not everyone can afford one, all right?"

"All right, all right," the tall guy replied as he pulled out his phone. "Don't bite my arm off. We'll do what we can to help you. Let's look up Halliday's here and see what we find."

As the three of them leaned in, peering at the phone, I inched my way over to the other end of the barricade. My heart pounded in my chest, and as I made it around to the other side and was about to start running toward the door, the tall guy turned and looked straight at me.

"Hey, there!" he yelled. "Just where do you think you're going?"

Chapter 11

KEEN: SHOWING EAGERNESS OR ENTHUSIASM

I kept running, down the narrow street, toward the faded red door. The shabby building really did look like something from long ago, with cracks in the building and sad, worn paint with big splotches of gray where the color had worn off entirely. But there was beauty there, too—around the entrance were panels of beautiful flowers and plants, all carved out of some kind of stone.

"Come back here!" one of the men yelled, footsteps stomping behind me, as I ran to the door and placed my hand, fingers spread, smack dab in the middle of it.

"What in heaven's name are you doing, young lady?" the short one said when he reached me.

"I just, uh, I wanted to see it," I said. "Up close. I've heard this place is really old and unique, and I was curious." I looked up as if to admire the place. "It's really splendid. Don't you agree?"

"I suppose it is, but you can't be here," he replied, while loud pounding noises rumbled from inside. "Come along now. Let's get you behind the barricade, where you belong."

He escorted me back to where the other worker and Ned still stood. The tall construction worker shook his head. "What'd you do that for?"

"She said she was curious," the other worker replied before I had a chance.

"Curious? About what? It's an old building, that's all."

"But it's been through a lot, hasn't it?" I asked. "Flooding, and the Blitz, I heard. What can you tell me about it? I want to know more."

The short one sighed. "If your mum would let you have a bloody phone, you could look it up yourselves."

The tall one chuckled. "He has very little patience. In case you didn't notice." He put his hand on to the barricade and leaned forward. "Let me tell you what I know about the place, since you're so keen on learning about it. I think it's great you have some interest in a fine piece of London history."

I smiled. "Thanks."

The short one gave a little harrumph while his co-worker began telling us what he knew. "In the mid eighteen hundreds, people came to see opera singers, circus acts, and ballet dancers. But then severe poverty hit the East End, and the East London Methodist Mission bought the place in 1888. At one point, the soup kitchen that was set up here served a thousand meals a day."

"Wow," Ned said. "So a lot of families were having a hard time."

"They certainly were. And then World War II happened. This place miraculously survived the Blitz—the only building in the vicinity to do so. Today, it's the world's last surviving grand music hall. Which is why it's wonderful that it's finally getting some desperately needed renovations."

"I wish I could see the inside," I said.

"No," the short one said, rapping his hand hard on the clipboard he held. "You cannot see the inside. Or even the outside up close. This is as far as you go. Now if you'll excuse us, we need to get back to work."

"Thank you for taking the time to answer our questions," Ned told them.

"You're welcome," the nice worker replied. "Happy to help."

After they left, I turned to Ned and smiled. "We did it! Thank you so much. Asking for directions to your grandparents' bookshop was brilliant."

"You're not very good at being sneaky, Pheebs," he said. "You should work on that. You never know when it'll come in handy."

"Oh, so you're the expert on being sneaky now, are you?" I asked with a smile. "What would you have done differently, then?"

"I would have crawled under the barrier, not gone around it."

I looked down and studied the plastic contraption. "Under it? Ned, the opening is barely big enough for a cat to crawl through. If you'd tried to do that, you would have gotten stuck."

"Nope," he said. "I could have done it."

"Do you have superpowers I don't know about?"

He wiggled his eyebrows. "Perhaps."

"Let me guess, you turn into a snake and slither around town, fighting crime."

"Boy, do I wish! Pheebs, that would be fantastic. Maybe I should let myself get bitten by a snake and see if it happens. You know, like Spiderman. He climbs walls like a spider. I could slither around the streets of London like a snake. I'd be so quick, so quiet, no one would see me coming."

I laughed. "You want to be Snakeman? That is funny, Ned." I pulled the letter out of my bag. "How about you use your superpowers to help me figure out where we go next? It says, *There are four corners of the square, but only three are occupied. Visit the empty space, place a coin, and make a wish.*"

He scoffed. "That's easy. So easy, you're probably thinking about it too hard."

I read it again, trying to figure out what it could possibly be.

"Parliament Square?" I asked.

"Nope. But you're on the right track."

I smile. "Oh! Trafalgar Square."

"That's the one. The fourth plinth doesn't have a permanent statue, remember? Back in Sheila's time, it was probably empty all the time. Not like now, where they put different pieces of artwork on it."

"The fourth what?"

"Plinth. That's what Mum calls them. You know, the pedestals where the statues stand? Sir Henry and King George. Can't remember the other guy."

"I like the bronze lions better than those stuffy old statues of men. Those should have been mentioned in the clue instead."

"Well, it doesn't matter that much, does it? We figured it out, that's the important thing. So let's go. And after that, can we get a bite to eat? I'm famished."

"Is there ever a time when you're *not* hungry, Ned?"

He thought about that for a moment before he replied, "Yes. When I'm sleeping."

Truer words were never spoken.

Chapter 12

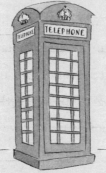

CHIPS: FRENCH FRIES

I've heard Trafalgar Square referred to as the heart of London. Lots of tourists visit the square every day, and I can see why. The National Gallery is nearby as well as the beautiful St. Martin-in-the-Fields church. Every December, a huge Christmas tree, given to us by Norway, is put up in the square. Dad told me once it's because they are thankful to Britain for helping them during World War II. The square is used for all kinds of celebrations, shows, and rallies. Last summer, Mum and Dad took Alice and me to a concert put on by the London Symphony Orchestra. It was free, which was good, but very crowded, which was annoying.

Along with the statues, there are fountains and the extremely tall Nelson's column, a monument that stands high in the air with Admiral Horatio Nelson at the very top. He was a naval hero who died at the Battle of Trafalgar.

When we arrived at the square, I was relieved to see there wasn't anything special going on. Just lots of tourists wandering around, like usual. As we crossed the street to enter, a horn from a nearby car went off, making me jump.

"Pheebs," Ned said, "look over there. At the fourth plinth."

"Can't you call it a pedestal?" I asked Ned. "It sounds like you're choking up a fur ball when you say that word."

He leaned down, close to my ear. "Plinth, plinth, plinth. PLINTH!"

I shoved him away and laughed. "Disgusting!"

I looked out, across the square at the thing Ned wanted me to see. "Wow," I said. "That is . . . something."

"I love it!" Ned said. "We should replace all of the stuffy old statues with more of those."

The piece of art now displayed on the fourth pedestal was a bright blue rooster. An extremely large blue rooster. It made me happy just looking at it.

When we reached the statue, we went around to the side, where there were some stairs, so we could get up closer to it.

"What would Sheila say if she could see that?" I asked, looking up.

"Maybe she has," Ned replied. "You never know."

I fished for the coin purse in my bag. "So where should I put the coin? I can't reach the pedestal. It's too tall."

"Plinth." Ned gave me a little smirk.

"Pedestal."

"Plinth."

"Okay, stop it. We could do this all day. And you want to go find some food, don't you? I'll get you a nice, big plate of chips once we're finished here."

Before Ned could reply, a whimpering sound came from around the corner, on the back side of the pedestal.

I looked at Ned. "Did you hear that?" I asked softly.

He nodded. I trotted up and around the corner to find a little boy with a head of curly, golden locks sitting by himself. He looked to be six or seven. "Hello, there. Is everything all right?"

He shook his head as he pressed his knees up closer to his chest, his arms wrapped tightly around them. I went over to him and crouched down. "Have you lost your mum?"

He looked at me, a scowl on his face. Like he wasn't sure if he should trust me or not.

"I lost my mum once," I told him. "In the Natural History Museum. Have you ever been there?"

He waited a second before he nodded his head.

"It's pretty neat, right? What's your favorite animal there?"

"The dinosaurs," he practically whispered.

"Ah, yes. The T. Rex has enormous teeth, doesn't he?" I took a seat on the step, because my knees were starting to hurt from crouching. "That day, when we were at the museum, I thought it'd be funny to hide from my sister and make her panic. But after I'd been hidden for a while, I got up and went to look for her and my mum, and I couldn't find them."

"Were you scared?" the boy asked. It was clear he was British, probably not one of the tourists.

Just then, Ned appeared. He took a seat on the steps nearby.

"Yes," I told the boy. "But a nice lady, who was a mother herself, helped me. She took me to the office, and someone called out my mum's name over the loudspeaker. Told her to come to the main office and collect her child." I chuckled. "Made it sound like I was a lost wallet or a set of keys or something."

"Was your mum mad?" the boy asked.

"Not really. She was just happy to find me. My sister, on the other hand, was completely annoyed with me. I got an earful from her. But that's what big sisters do, I guess."

"I don't have any brothers or sisters," the boy said. "I wish I did sometimes. I'm the only one my mother has to worry about." He blinked his eyes, like he was trying hard not to cry. "She's going to be so mad."

"You're here with your mother, then?" Ned asked.

"Yes. And my aunt and uncle, who're from Liverpool."

"We can help you find them if you'd like," I said. "But first, can you tell us your name?"

"Archie."

"Nice to meet you, Archie," I said, holding my hand out. After he shook it, I said, "I'm Phoebe and this is my friend Ned."

"So what's the plan?" Ned asked me as he got up.

Both Archie and I stood up as well. "We're going to make a wish that we'll find his family," I announced. "And then we'll stand smack-dab in the middle of the square and hope they spot us. Sometimes you simply have to believe things will work out, even when you don't know for sure that they will. And, as I told my friend Nora once, whatever will be, will be."

I took a coin out of my pouch and placed it on a step, underneath the blue rooster. "I wish that Archie's family will find us straight away." I looked at Archie and winked at him. "And that his mother is not annoyed with him like my sister was with me when I became lost."

As we headed down the steps, Archie asked, "How come your sister's not with you?"

"She and I are having . . . sisterly difficulties."

"What's that mean?" he asked.

"It means they're not getting along very well," Ned said.

"Sorry," Archie said as we brushed past people walking through the square. A man with a cowboy hat, cowboy boots, and a big, shiny belt buckle stood out almost more than the blue rooster did. A visiting American, no doubt.

"It's all right," I said with a smile. "I'm hoping things get better soon."

Archie wiped the hair out of his eyes. "Maybe she's jealous of you."

I laughed. "Of me? I highly doubt that."

"A boy at school wasn't being very nice to me. During reading time, I'd be sitting on the special carpet, reading to myself, and he'd come over and kick me or poke me with his pencil. Mum said he was probably jealous because I could read and he couldn't. Just looking at the pictures is boring. So one day I asked him if he wanted to read a book together."

"And what happened?" I asked.

He shrugged. "He said yes. And now we're friends."

A moment after he finished his story, we heard a woman's voice shrieking through the air. "Archie! Archie, there you are!"

We turned to see two women and a man sprinting toward us.

Archie started running, and when he reached his mum, she swooped down and threw her arms around him. When they let go of each other, Archie pointed our way as he probably explained how we had helped him.

"Thank you!" his mum called out, waving at us.

We waved back. "Bye, Archie!" I called out.

"Nice meeting you!" Ned yelled.

"Bye!" Archie replied.

And with that, the four of them went on their way.

"Your wish came true," Ned said.

I looked over at the blue rooster. "I'm so glad. I love a happy ending. I had planned on wishing for something different, but it seemed like Archie was more important at the moment."

Ned pulled out his phone to check the time. "You did the right thing, Pheebs."

I was about to suggest we go find a place to get some chips when Ned's phone rang. "Hello? Oh, hi, Mum. No, we were just about to go and—"

He looked down at the ground as he listened. The expression on his face looked sadder and sadder. Once in a while, he'd try to protest something that was being said, but it was like he couldn't get a word in edgewise. Finally, he said, "All right. See you soon."

"What is it?" I asked. "What's wrong?"

"I have to go home."

"But we're not finished yet."

"I know. I'm sorry. But I didn't clean my room, and my mum is furious with me. I was supposed to do it before I left this morning."

"Ned, but I can't wander around London by myself."

"Well, you could, actually. Your parents would never know, right? I'm sure you'd be fine."

"But I don't want to. Can't you get her to change her mind?"

He shook his head. "Sorry, Pheebs. I have to go home."

This was horrible. We'd only accomplished three things on the list. I looked around, trying to decide what to do.

"Maybe she'll let me go again tomorrow," Ned suggested. "What do you say?"

"My mother barely let me go today," I said with a sigh. "I'm not sure what she'll say if I ask to come back to London with you tomorrow."

"All you can do is try," he said as he began walking. I trudged along after him. "And remember what you told Archie—whatever will be, will be!"

Why does advice always sound so much better coming from yourself rather than someone else?

Chapter 13

HUNKY-DORY: EXCELLENT

When I walked through the door, Mum was happy to see me. I'd texted to let her know I was on my way, but it was like she still expected me to meet some horrible fate before returning safely home.

"Phoebe!" she said, rushing to greet me, a big smile on her face. "Did you have a nice time with Ned?"

"Yes. Up until the point where he had to go home because he forgot to clean his room."

"Oh no," she said. "Were you able to find a gift for his mother before he had to go?"

"No. He asked if we could meet up again tomorrow."

I hated not being a hundred percent honest with her, but what else was I supposed to do? I had to keep the story going for now. "Do you think that'd be all right?"

She scowled. "I thought you, me, and Alice might do something together. I work this evening for a while, but I have tomorrow free."

"But, Mum—"

She just patted my shoulder and took off toward the kitchen. "Let me think on it a bit, Phoebe. We'll talk it over later. For now, will you come along and help me make some lunch?"

I sighed. "All right. Let me put my bag away."

When I entered my room, I couldn't have been more shocked if a chimpanzee jumped out to greet me. My entire desk was in shambles—papers thrown on the floor, my box of colored pencils spilled all over the carpet, and every single drawer open.

I threw my bag on my bed and screamed, "Alice!" as I did an about-face and headed toward her room. I could feel my cheeks getting hotter with every step.

Her door was closed. I went to push it open, but it was locked. I pounded on it with both fists. "Open up right now."

When nothing happened, I stopped pounding and listened. I could hear the radio playing but not loudly. And then I heard her voice, followed by a laugh.

Was she talking on the phone? Was she *laughing* at me?

"What in the world is going on?" Mum asked from behind me. "Phoebe? Is everything all right?"

Tears stung my eyes. "Oh sure. Hunky-dory." I spun around. "Alice went into my room and made a mess, all because I told her to wait until I got home for me to find Nora and Justin's address."

Mum went down the hall and peeked her head into my room. When she turned around and came back to me, the look on her face told me she was about as angry as I was.

This time, she knocked. "Alice, unlock this door right now."

A moment later, it opened, with my sister standing there looking extremely annoyed. "What?"

"You have some explaining to do. Why did you do that to Phoebe's room?"

"Mum, don't you dare take her side on this. She could have easily told me where to find the address, but she refused. She thinks this whole thing with Justin is ridiculous, so she wanted to hurt me when I asked her to tell me where I could find it."

"That is not true!" I said. It was becoming more and more difficult to keep the tears back. "I didn't want you in my stuff. And, wow, I wonder why?"

"Alice, there is no excuse for leaving her room in such a state," Mum said, looking quite cross. "You need to apologize and help your sister clean up her room."

"After she gives me the address, I will gladly help her clean up."

I scoffed before I replied, "You think you're getting that now, after what you've done?"

Alice narrowed her eyes. "Where is it?"

"Wouldn't you like to know?"

She lunged for me, but I ran to my room and slammed the door. I leaned up against it, my chest heaving as I looked at the mess again, and the tears started to fall.

And this time, I didn't stop them.

"Phoebe?" It was Mum.

"Can I be alone for a little while?" I sniffled. "Please?"

It was quiet for a moment before she said, "All right. Can I bring you a sandwich to eat? You must be hungry."

I had no appetite whatsoever, but I knew she wouldn't take no for an answer. "Not now. Maybe in a while?"

"All right."

I heard her voice, softer now, talking to Alice. I leaned my ear to the door. "Give her some time to cool off, and then you need to apologize."

"She better give me that address," Alice replied.

I glanced over at *Harry Potter and the Chamber of Secrets* on my bookshelf and smiled. I'd tucked the sheet of paper with Nora's information in between the pages when we returned from Paris, because both Nora and I are huge fans of the series.

I knew Harry would keep my secret safe. Because for now, that piece of paper was staying put.

Chapter 14

KERFUFFLE: A SKIRMISH, FIGHT, OR ARGUMENT

I texted Ned after I cleaned up the mess myself. The last thing I wanted was my sister in my room again.

Me: Did you get your room clean?

Ned: Working on it.

Me: You're not done yet???

Ned: Cleaning is so boring. Plus I'm hungry. Time for tea and biscuits.

Me: You better finish. I think my mum will let me go again tomorrow.

Ned: That's good! How come?

Me: Because my sister is horrible and rotten to me. And my mum feels bad.

Ned: Well, hooray for rotten and horrible sisters, then. Are you sure you want this spell to work, if she is truly that awful?

It was a good question. I had to think for a second before I responded.

Me: She needs me in her life. I think that might be why she is so horrible.

Ned: Makes sense. Let me know what time to meet you. Going to eat something now. Wait. Scratch that. I'm going to go back to cleaning now.

Me: Sure you are. See you tomorrow.

I put the phone down and realized I was famished. I hadn't eaten anything since breakfast. Just as I was about to leave the safe and secure walls of my room, there was a tap at the door.

"Who is it?" I called out.

"Me," said my mum's sweet voice. "I've brought you some food. Figured you must be hungry by now."

I couldn't get to the door fast enough. "Thank you," I said as I opened the door. She had a tray with a tuna sandwich and some crisps, along with a glass of juice. "You can set it on my desk, since it's back to normal."

"I'm so sorry about that kerfuffle with your sister. I

don't know what has gotten into her lately. Maybe she's anxious about university. Or—"

"It doesn't matter," I said as I picked up half of my sandwich and took a bite.

"It most certainly does," she replied.

I finished swallowing before I said, "No, I mean, it doesn't matter what's causing it. It's impossible to know for sure, isn't it? So it doesn't make sense to try and guess."

She sat down on my bed. "But Phoebe, if there's a reason, I think it would help you feel better. It'd certainly help *me* feel better." She sighed. "I asked her, you know. A little while ago. I asked her if there was something she'd like to talk to me about. If something might be troubling her. And all she said was that she's just really sad about Justin being so far away."

I rolled my eyes as I nibbled on my sandwich some more. "Lovesick. That's what I keep saying."

"Hm. Maybe that is all it is. If so, time is probably the only cure. In the meantime, I suppose we try to be as understanding as possible."

"And keep a padlock on my bedroom door?" I asked.

"She's going to apologize for that," Mum said. "Coming in here and going through your things was wrong, and you have every right to be angry with her."

My sister's ears must have been burning, because just then she popped her head into the room. "Can I come in?"

"Please do," Mum said. That was not the answer I would have given if my mum hadn't been there. Mine would have been something like, "Enter at your own risk."

"I'm sorry, Phoebe," she said softly. "I shouldn't have cluttered your room like that. But I was angry. It felt like you were keeping the address from me on purpose."

I munched on my crisps. As long as my mouth was full, I couldn't say anything mean that I might regret. Fortunately, my mother spoke logically for the both of us. "Your sister asked you to wait until she got home, and you should have done that, love," Mum said. "You know what I've always said."

"I know, I know. Patience is a virtue," Alice replied. "You might like to know I didn't really understand what that meant until recently."

I looked at my mother. "What *does* it mean, exactly?"

She smiled. "It means patience is a wonderful quality to possess."

Alice sighed as she fiddled with the doorknob, like she was nervous. "Lately, it feels like I'm waiting for everything. It's a terrible feeling. Like nothing right now is any good, it's all in the future."

Mum looked at me and winked. Like this was what she was talking about earlier, when she said maybe there was something causing Alice's obnoxious behavior. But I didn't get it, because there was stuff right now that was good. Like me, her fun and wonderful sister, sitting *right in front of her*!

"Anyway, Phoebe," Alice continued, "may I please have Justin's address?"

I bit my lip as I considered her request. "How about I give it to you tomorrow? Waiting a bit longer can be your punishment for what you did to my room."

"Mum!" she whined. "That's not fair."

"I think it's perfectly fair," Mum said. "What you did was wrong. And so you'll get it tomorrow."

Alice was about to argue some more when her phone started ringing. She popped that thing out of her pocket so fast, I wondered if she had magical abilities. But of course she didn't. It was simply a side effect of the love-sickness. It might be Justin calling her, after all.

"It's Kiera," Alice said. "I should take this." She looked at me. "You win. I'll get it from you tomorrow. So we're good, yes?"

Of course, in typical Alice fashion, she didn't wait for my reply—just ducked out of the room and that was that.

Mum stood up, a big smile on her face. "That was nice, wasn't it? She apologized and told us how she's feeling. It makes sense now, doesn't it, Pheebs?"

I felt like they'd been speaking a language I didn't understand, because it didn't make any sense to me. But I decided I didn't want to talk about it anymore. So I tried my best to smile and replied with a simple, "Yep."

"Wonderful," she said. "Finish your sandwich, and then maybe we can work on that jigsaw puzzle Dad brought home from the shop. How's that sound?"

"Fine, I suppose."

Even though the last thing I needed was one more puzzle in my life.

Chapter 15

DODGY: SUSPICIOUS

When supper was almost over, I decided it was time to try again. "Mum, since our trip into London was cut short, can Ned and I go again tomorrow? Please?"

Alice scowled at me. I ignored her and continued looking at Mum, who balled up her napkin, placed it on the empty plate, and leaned back in her chair. Like she was carefully considering this request, even though she'd had hours to think about it. After everything that had happened that afternoon, I honestly thought this would be an easy question for her to answer. Not only did I think I deserved a bit of kindness after what Alice had done to my room, but I also believed Mum would see that maybe it was best to keep us apart as much as possible for the rest of our break. Although once the spell worked its magic, it wouldn't be as much of an issue for us to be around one another. At least, I hoped that would be the case.

"I don't think she should go," Alice said as she picked at a pea with her fork. "The whole thing sounds dodgy to me. How do we know what she's up to, exactly?"

I turned and stared at my sister the way a teacher stares at a student who has been very, very naughty. "Be quiet," I told her. "This is none of your business."

Mum looked at Dad with a sigh. Dad looked at Alice. "I think Phoebe is right. You need to stay out of this discussion."

I wanted to kiss my dad in that moment, while Alice looked like she might want to poke him with her fork.

"Please?" I said again. "Ned is really counting on me. And everything went fine today, didn't it?"

"I suppose it did," Mum said. She looked at my dad. "Is it all right with you?"

"Yes," he said as he stood up, his plate in his hand. "Now, who is going to help me with the dishes?" He stared at Alice but she stood up and handed him her plate.

"Sorry. Can't. Heading over to Kiera's for a while."

She went to the coat closet and grabbed a jacket. "Be home by eleven," Mum called out.

Alice didn't reply. In fact, she didn't even say good-bye. Just walked out the door like she was Queen Elizabeth on her way to a jubilee.

"That's it?" I asked as I stood up. "No questions about what she'll be doing or anything?"

"What is there to ask, Pheebs?" Dad replied as he picked up Mum's plate as well. "She's going to her best friend's house, where she's been hundreds of times."

"Yes," Mum said. "It's quite different from what you're doing with Ned. Please don't be upset with us for worrying about you. We're your parents. We have to make sure you're safe, you see?"

"But sometimes you make me feel like I'm a small, helpless child. And I'm not."

Mum stood up from her spot next to me and rubbed my back. "We know you're not, lovey. Believe us, we know all too well. You are growing up into a fine young woman and we understand you want to spread your wings. But we were just as protective with Alice when she was your age. You simply don't remember, that's all."

"Phoebe, will you come along and help me with the dishes while Mum gets ready for work?" Dad said. "I want to hear about your morning around London."

I gulped as my mind raced, trying to figure out what I should tell him. After I picked up my plate and silverware, I said, "We came across a lost boy and had to help him find his family."

Dad looked at me with his eyes wide before he turned toward the kitchen. "Now that sounds like a fascinating story."

Hopefully, I could stretch it out to last a good, long while, so I wouldn't have to tell him all of the other things Ned and I did involving a very secret letter.

Once the kitchen was clean, I went to the piano and played for twenty minutes or so. It had kind of been a stressful day, and playing always helps me to relax. When I finished, I went to my room and grabbed a blue notecard, because I wanted to remember the one truly great thing that had happened that day.

Maybe we didn't get to do all of the things to complete the spell, but at least we did help a little boy. It was the highlight of the day, for sure. Dad said we did a great thing, and even if Archie was too young to truly appreciate that now, someday he would. After all, who knows how long he would have stayed hidden in that corner spot, beneath the giant blue rooster.

After I texted Ned that tomorrow I'd meet him at the same time, same place, I went to my bookshelf and pulled out the piece of paper with Nora and Justin's address. Part of me still wanted to keep it hidden away, to make Alice hurt because she'd hurt me lately with her comments and obnoxious behavior. But the other part knew it was best to hand it over. After all, I'd told her I would. And sometimes, as hard as it might be, I knew it was best to be nice. Even when it was really, *really* hard.

I sat at my desk and wrote Alice a note and included Justin's address. Then, I decided I'd be extra nice and give it to her tonight instead of tomorrow. I took it to her bedroom and taped it to the outside of her door, so she'd see it when she came home.

Then I went back to my room and wrote Nora a postcard, telling her about my last days in Paris where I met a nice girl named Cherry and found a lovely antique. There wasn't much room for details, but I wanted her to know I was thinking about her and missing her. Our time in Paris together had been so much fun. If only she could be here to help me go around London and do the items in the letter.

Good old Ned would have to do. Though I bet if Nora were here, she wouldn't have had to go home early because of a dirty room.

Chapter 16

HOOVER: VACUUM

So where are we going?" Ned asked when I met up with him at the Tube station. His hair was messy and his windbreaker was buttoned up wrong.

"Are you all right?" I asked, pointing to his jacket.

"Tired," he said, stifling a yawn. Then he looked up at the sky. "We might get wet today. Mum said it's supposed to rain later."

"Then we should hurry. Before the rain comes."

"Where to first?" Ned asked as he redid his buttons.

"I'm not sure. There are probably quite a few churches with clocks and steeples."

"But how many of them have crypts?" he asked.

"That I don't know," I replied. "And I'm not sure how we find out without visiting them all. We don't have time to do that."

"Maybe you should just pick one and hope it's the right one."

"And risk the magic not working because of that one wrong move?" I shook my head. "No. We have to get it right. If you'd seen Alice yesterday afternoon, the way I did, you'd understand why it's more important than ever that we get this done properly."

"Let's work through the possibilities," said Ned. "As if we're detectives."

"All right. Name a church."

"Westminster Abbey."

"Can't be that one," I replied. "It doesn't have a steeple, really. More like . . . towers."

"All right. How about the Strand in Westminster?"

"I've never been there. It has a clock?"

"Yes."

"Well," I said, recalling where we were yesterday, "I think it must be St. Martin-in-the-Fields."

He looked at me curiously. "Why do you think that?"

"Because it's in Trafalgar Square, the same place we were yesterday. Go to the empty pedestal—"

"Plinth."

"Whatever, and then hop across the street to the church. It makes sense, doesn't it?"

"But Pheebs, if it's a spell, how close or far apart the places are from one another doesn't matter. It's how they all work together to create the magic." He scratched his head. "At least, I think so?"

Suddenly, I was worried. How could we know for sure which one was the right one? And it didn't seem like we had time to go to both.

I pulled out my phone.

"What are you doing?"

"Texting Dad. I'm going to ask him if St. Martin has a crypt."

Ned scowled. "Isn't that using technology? Something we agreed we wouldn't do?"

I looked around at the people who were nearby in the station. I could have asked one of them, but asking my dad would be so much quicker. One of the things he'd taught me about antiques shopping is that every situation is different, and a good shopper will size up the opportunity and do what's best under the circumstances. Like, if you know a certain vendor is tough to deal with and doesn't let things go for cheap, offering up a really low price is not going to be very smart. Of course, you can't always know what might work best, but if you do, you have to make the most of it.

And right now, what I knew for sure was that we didn't have any time to waste.

"Just this once. Please?" I pleaded with Ned.

He let out a harrumph. "Fine. But only because we need to finish this up so we can move on to the thing *I* need help with—finding my mother the perfect birthday gift."

I sent the text and waited. The train came so we hopped on, and I crossed my fingers Dad would reply soon so we could figure out what stop we needed. A moment later, it came through.

"What's it say?" Ned asked.

I read it aloud. "*Yes, there's a crypt at St. Martin. Robert Boyle, a pioneer chemist, is buried there. I've never heard of anyone shopping at a crypt for a birthday gift. Sure that's wise? Be safe. I'm going to hoover the shop now.*"

Ned smiled. "Your dad is funny."

"At least he didn't ask me why I wanted to know. Not sure what I would have said. I really don't like lying to them about this."

He leaned back in his seat and crossed his arms. "You could tell them what you're doing, you know. They might get a kick out of it."

"I don't think so," I said. "I think they'd say it's silly. Childish. Besides, when I say we're going into London to find your mum a birthday present, I'm not *really* lying, am I? We are going to do that. Eventually."

"I suppose you're right." He leaned back even more and closed his eyes. "Now if you don't mind, I think I'll catch a few winks before we get to our stop. Wake me when we get there, will you?"

"Ned, you can't do that."

He scowled at me. "Why not?"

"Because we're in this together. And we need to figure out where we go after St. Martin."

"I'm sure you can figure it out on your own. Just a few minutes, Pheebs. I'm so very tired."

With that, he rolled his head over to the side and closed his eyes. And I pulled Sheila's letter out of my pocket, and read it for about the fiftieth time.

Chapter 17

WONKY: NOT RIGHT

$\mathcal{S}$ince St. Martin is open to the public, walking through the door while holding my breath wasn't a challenge at all. I walked in, I walked out, and that was that. It's a glorious old church, with huge columns along the front and blue-faced clocks that adorn the steeple on every side. As I looked for Ned, I wondered if it looked the same when Sheila was here. Had it been harmed during the war at all? To me it looked like it had stood a thousand years, strong and true, and could stand a thousand more.

Ned was leaning against one of the stone pillars, looking pale. "Are you all right?" I asked.

"I don't know," he said. "Feeling a bit . . . wonky."

"Do you need something to eat?" I asked. "I bet that would make you feel better. There must be a place around here where we can pop in and get you a little snack."

He shook his head. "No. I don't want anything to eat. Let's just get on with your spell. Where to next?"

Now I was even more concerned. "You don't want to eat? Ned, that is not a good sign."

He pushed himself away from the pillar. "I'm fine. Now, what's the clue again?"

I pulled out the list and read the fifth item. *"Blow a kiss through the window of the Indian restaurant where Winston Churchill once dined."*

"We're never going to figure that one out on our own," Ned said. "We need to ask someone."

"But who?" I wondered, turning and staring out at the mass of people in the square. "We need someone who knows London *really* well."

"Yes," Ned agreed. "That's going to be the difficult part. I bet a lot of these people are tourists."

I searched the crowd until I saw an elderly couple walking slowly up the steps toward the church. I nodded my head toward them. "There. Let's give them a try."

A lot of older people like to come into our shop, hoping to find vintage items they grew up with. My friend Kiki was at the shop once and Dad was busy with someone, so I stepped over to help an elderly couple. They'd been looking for an old hand eggbeater. "One with a wooden handle," the woman had said. "It has to have a wooden handle. It's much more comfortable to hold than one made of all metal."

I ended up talking with the couple for a while, because they were so nice. After they left, Kiki had said to me, "You were so good with them. I've never told anyone this, but old people kind of scare me."

I must have looked at her like she'd admitted she didn't like sweets. "But it's not like they're spiders with eight legs or something creepy like that. They're just people."

"I know," she'd said. "I know it's strange." She'd looked so ashamed, and I instantly felt bad for making her feel bad.

"I'm sorry," I'd told her. "It's hard when you're afraid of something other people might not be understand. The thing is, someday we'll be old, too. Maybe if you think of that, it'll help you relate to them a little more?

Like, imagine you're talking to me, just seventy years from now."

She'd smiled. "Hey, that's a great idea."

As I approached this elderly couple on the stairs of the church, I remembered my own advice. I pretended I was about to talk to Ned and myself seventy years from now. And of course, we wouldn't mind being asked for help.

"Excuse me," I said. "Hello. My friend and I are wondering if you happen to know London very well?"

"Lived here for over eighty years," the woman replied in a soft, husky voice. "Do you need help finding something?"

"Yes," I replied. "We have a puzzle we're trying to solve. We're supposed to find the Indian restaurant where Winston Churchill ate."

The old man looked at his wife. "What's the name of that place? Do you remember?"

"Have we eaten there?" she asked.

"I think so. Haven't we?" He paused. "Yes, we've been there. We ran into your friend. The one who always wears the funny hats. What's her name?"

"Gladys?"

"Yes, that's right. Gladys."

I glanced over at Ned, and he raised his eyebrows as if to say, "Isn't this fun?" And actually, I thought it was. Old people are cute, poor memories and all.

They both stopped talking as if they couldn't quite remember what they'd been discussing before Gladys. But then the old man remembered.

"The restaurant. What's the name? It's not far from here. I think it starts with a *V*."

"*T*?" she asks.

"No, *V*."

By now, Ned was no doubt wishing he'd just let me text my dad like I did for the last clue. But it was too late to back out now.

For a moment, they were quiet, thinking, and I held my breath as I waited to see if one of them would finally come up with the name. When the woman said, "I've got it! It's Veeraswamy," I let out a sigh of relief.

"Oh, thank you both so much," I said.

Ned extended his hand to the old man, and he took it. "Yes, thank you. You said it's not far from here. Is it close enough to walk?"

"Most definitely," the old man said. "Go through Odeon Leicester Square to Coventry Street, and after a couple of blocks, you'll want to get onto Regent Street.

Should only take you about ten minutes or so to get there. Maybe less, since the two of you probably walk a whole lot faster than we do."

The woman looked at her gold wristwatch. "It's early," she said. "They may not be open yet."

"And if it is open," the man chimed in, "it's rather expensive. Are you sure you have enough to pay for a meal there?"

"We're not going to eat there," I explained. "We just want to see it."

The woman smiled. "Brilliant. Well, enjoy yourselves, then. And do be safe walking over that way."

"We will," Ned replied. "Don't worry. Thank you again."

"Good-bye!" I called out as I skipped down the steps. But when I got to the bottom of the stairs, I realized Ned wasn't next to me. I turned around to find him walking very slowly toward me. The old couple probably could have walked faster if they'd been going this way.

"What's the matter?" I called up to him.

"Horrible stomachache," he said.

"Do you think you can make it to the restaurant?"

He stopped and stared out at the city. "I hope so, Pheebs. That's all I can say. I hope so."

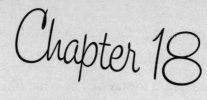

Chapter 18

LIFT: ELEVATOR

It took us an hour, although it should have taken a fraction of the time. Ned kept having to stop and rest. *Where is Snakeman when you need him?* was what I wanted to know. Once we finally saw the signs, I was really worried about him.

"I think after this, we need to get you home," I told him as he wiped the glistening beads of sweat from his forehead.

"But I haven't shopped for my mum's gift yet," he said. "And we're running out of time."

"It's Wednesday," I replied. "You still have two whole days. The party isn't until Friday afternoon, right?"

"I know, but . . ."

He really didn't look very good at all. And as much as I wanted him to stay and help me finish the tasks for the list, I knew he needed to get home. I walked a little farther up the sidewalk to the bright purple sign that said VEERASWAMY, but something wasn't right. The flag hung above a shoe store. And next to it was a clothing store. Regent Street was filled with shop after shop, but there was no restaurant here that I could see.

So where was it?

Ned joined me and asked, "What's going on?"

"How come it's not here?" I asked. "Why is there a flag hung above a shoe shop?"

Ned backed up and looked around. "I bet it's on the second floor. You must enter around the side or something." He pointed to a big archway down the sidewalk a little bit. "Maybe there are stairs or a lift around the corner, to get you up to the restaurant."

"Wait here," I told him before I scurried over to where he'd been pointing. When I saw that he was correct, I let out a huge sigh of relief.

I returned to Ned and looked at the windows on the second floor. "So I blow a kiss up there, then?" I asked.

"I suppose you do," he said.

I imagined Sheila, standing in this spot doing the same thing. Did it feel as strange to her as it did to me? I looked around and waited until there was a break in the people passing by us before I put my hands to my lips, let out a kiss, and blew it up to those windows.

Ned glanced down the street. "There are lots of shops here, Phoebe. We should go in some of them. See if we can find something for my mum."

"Do you feel up to it?" I asked.

"Not really. But I need to get it taken care of."

I looked down the sidewalk, hoping there might be a bench we could sit on for a bit, but there wasn't a single place to rest.

"Do you want to get her some shoes?" I teased, looking at the shop right in front of us.

"Too expensive," he said. "Besides, I wouldn't know her size."

I was about to reply when he mumbled, "Uh-oh." He stumbled backward a couple of steps, turned around, and vomited at the base of a lamppost.

"Ew," I whispered as I glanced around. A few people looked at us with pity on their faces. This couldn't be happening. My friend was not getting sick on the streets of London. So horrifying! The only thing that would have made it even more horrifying was if Kate Middleton herself showed up at that moment to do a bit of shoe shopping.

I couldn't bear the thought. I also couldn't go near Ned and the . . . mess.

He leaned up against the lamppost for a few minutes while I paced up and down the sidewalk. Finally, he said, "I need to go home, Phoebe. I'm sorry."

"Don't be sorry," I said, my back to him. "I shouldn't have made you walk all that way. And now we have to get to the Tube."

"You should stay," he said, coming up to me as he reached into his pocket and pulled out a pack of gum. He popped a piece into his mouth before he offered me one.

"Glad you brought gum along today instead of your compass," I told him.

"See? I don't always do things that make absolutely no sense." I smiled as he asked, "What's next on the list?"

"A cemetery. One where songbirds apparently sing. I have no idea where that might be."

"Once you figure it out, you could go there by yourself," he said. "You're already out and about, and your family won't be expecting you for a while."

"Ned, you're ill. I can't leave you alone like that. What if you pass out or something? I'd feel awful. No, we have to get you home, straight away."

"Are you sure?"

"Absolutely positively."

"But what if you don't get a chance to finish everything?" Ned asked as we walked down the sidewalk. "What if this is your one and only chance?"

I felt my stomach lurch at the thought. We'd come so far and there were only two places left to visit. It couldn't be over now. It just couldn't be.

"What's the place after the cemetery?" Ned asked as he rubbed his stomach slightly. "I've forgotten."

"The tea shop. I'm sure it's Twinings. There's a gold lion statue above the doorway, remember?"

Ned stopped. "I wonder how far it is from here?"

"Why?"

"Because we could do that one. Before we go. Then all you have left is the cemetery to visit."

"But you're in no condition to walk, and if I remember

correctly, it's quite far from here. Besides, up to this point, I've done everything in order. What if I mess everything up?"

He smiled. "You're not going to mess anything up. Does it state anywhere they *have* to be done in order?"

I shook my head *no*.

"I think it will be fine. We'll take a taxi and you can hop out and do what you need to do. When you're finished, we'll have the driver take us to the nearest Tube station."

"I'm not sure I have enough money to do that, though."

"I'll help you pay," he said. "I'll use some of the money I set aside for the birthday gift." He took a deep breath. "I really need to sit down, Pheebs. Trust me. This is the best thing for both of us."

"But the money. You can't spend it on me. It's for your mum!"

"Yes, I can," he said. "Because in the next couple of days, you're going to help me find something fabulous. And extremely inexpensive."

Before I could protest, Ned had stepped to the curb and hailed a black London cab. When it stopped, Ned reached out and opened the door. "Your chariot awaits, my lady."

This day was not going at all like I had planned. Still, there was nothing to do but hop in and see what would happen next.

Chapter 19

POUNDS: THE UK UNIT OF CURRENCY

As we pulled up near Twinings Tea Shop, it began to rain. Ned asked the driver to pull over and let me out.

"What about some tea for your mum?" I asked Ned. "I could get a sample pack or something fun like that."

He shook his head. "No, thanks. Too boring. I want something really special."

"What if you got a new teacup to go with it?"

He thought about it for a moment before he shook his head again. That was it, then. Tea was out.

"Ned's going to stay and I'll be right back," I told the driver. He was an old man with glasses and a beard and hadn't said a word since we'd gotten into the car. Even now, he simply nodded, letting me know he understood.

The fare was already up to over ten pounds and the thought of it going much higher made *my* stomach hurt. I had to hurry. The instructions said I was to leave a gift in the hollow pillar. As I rushed toward the shop, rain-drops splattering on me, I searched my bag for something I could leave as a gift.

A bobby pin?

A tube of lip gloss?

And then, my hand struck something. When I had picked up a postcard to send to Nora, I'd purchased an extra one, just in case I made a mistake while writing my note. I pulled it out along with a pen. Once I reached the tiny entrance to the shop, I ducked under the small awning and wrote this on the back of the postcard:

Here's hoping the magic works!
~ Phoebe

I felt around the right-hand column first, but didn't find any place that might open to reveal a hollow space. I couldn't reach all the way to the top, but I figured no one probably could, so it wouldn't be up there. When I moved to the left-hand column, I found a little latch at the base of the column. It was stuck, though. As I tried to push it open, an old lady wearing a pink hat walked by and asked, "Is everything all right down there?"

"Yes, quite all right," I replied as I quickly stood up. "I've dropped something and I'm trying to find it."

"Would you like me to help you?"

"No, I can manage. Thank you, though."

She gave me a strange look. "All right, then. Good luck."

Once she was gone, I crouched down again and pushed on the latch as hard as I could. This time, it gave way—just a tiny bit at first, and then as I kept at it, more and more. But when I tried to place the postcard into the space, it got stuck on something and wouldn't go in all the way. It seemed as if there was another object blocking the space, so I poked two fingers in there, and sure enough, the hole wasn't empty. It felt like a small box, and once I pried the opening a little wider, I was able to pull it out.

A silver box with a gold ribbon wrapped around it! The box was in perfect condition, which made sense, I suppose. It had been stuck inside that hollow column where it was safe from sunlight, air, and even moisture, it seemed. I glanced across the street, at the taxi waiting for me, and I knew no matter how badly I wanted to open it to see what was inside, I'd do it when I got home. As much as I adored Ned and was thankful he was with me, I wanted to open the box in private.

I stuck the postcard into the hole and closed it back up tight. Then I stuffed the little box into my bag before running back to the taxi.

When I plopped down next to Ned, I swept my hair off of my face and let out a big sigh. "To the nearest Tube station," I told the driver.

He gave a quick nod before he pulled into traffic.

"Did you do what you needed to do?" Ned asked me.

"Yes. I had a bit of trouble opening the tiny latch, that's why it took so long."

"I saw that woman stop and talk to you. What'd she say?"

I smiled. "She wondered what in the world I was doing down there, near the ground. I told her I'd dropped something and was trying to find it."

"Good thinking," he replied as he leaned his head back and closed his eyes.

"Ned? Are you all right?"

"I'm tired. And my stomach is starting to hurt again."

"Oh no. Try and hang on for a little while longer, will you?"

"I wish we had enough money to take this cab all the way home."

"I know," I replied, leaning my head back as well. "But we don't."

"Too bad."

"Yep."

"Phoebe?"

"Hm?"

"What am I going to get my mum for her birthday?"

With a sigh, I responded, "You should have let me get her some tea, Ned. Everyone loves tea."

"You'll think of something else, won't you?"

I didn't have an answer for that.

Chapter 20

TELLY: **TELEVISION**

"Hi, Phoebe," Mum called out from the kitchen when she heard the front door shut. "Want some lunch? Alice and I already ate, but there's some soup I can quickly heat up for you."

"Sure," I said. "Can you wait like five minutes?"

For some reason, that response must have alarmed her because she appeared before me a moment later. "Everything all right?" she asked, eyeing me up and down.

I smiled. "Fine. I just want to change into some dry clothes. It's raining and I got wet walking home."

Relief washed over her face. "Oh, of course. Sure thing. Clean yourself up and then come find me. I'll sit with you while you eat so I can hear all about your adventure today." She turned to leave but stopped. "You're home awfully early, aren't you? Did you find a gift fairly quickly, then?"

"No," I grumbled. "Ned got sick. It was horrible. He threw up on the sidewalk."

Mum's face scrunched up. "Oh no! I'm so sorry. I hope he's well enough by Friday to go to the party."

"Me too," I replied.

She rubbed my arm. "All right, run along and I'll see you in a bit."

She didn't have to tell me twice. Then, of course, I had to run into Alice in the hallway.

"Back already?" she asked.

"Obviously," was my bratty reply. What was happening to me? She'd turned me into a horrible person.

Horrible!

"Ned wasn't feeling well," I said, my voice gentler. "So we had to come back early. I feel so bad for him. Two days in London, and he still doesn't have a birthday gift for his mum."

"Time to get creative," she said as she walked toward her room.

"What are you doing today?" I asked. I wanted to ask if she might like to bake some cookies or something, but the fear of rejection stopped me.

"I sent the package off to Justin," she said. "I hope he likes it. With that out of the way, I think I might watch the telly this afternoon while I paint my nails. Rainy day activities, you know?"

I waited for her to ask if I might want to join her. But nothing came next.

"What color?"

"Huh?"

"What color are you going to paint your nails?"

This was a running joke of ours. We used to love coming up with funny nail polish colors. Runny Nose Red, Pretty in Parmesan Cheese, and Dandy Dead Dandelions were just a few of the names we'd come up with.

She shrugged. "I don't know. I haven't decided yet. Probably blue."

I wanted to make her laugh so badly. It never used to be difficult. In fact, it happened so much, it wasn't even something I thought about. But here I was, thinking about it, and I knew this was my chance to get a little of the old Alice back. The problem was, when the pressure is on, it's hard to be funny.

"Frozen Toes Blue?" I asked.

She didn't even crack a smile. Just stared at me and didn't say a word.

"I was trying to be funny," I explained. "Don't you remember? Runny Nose Red?"

She headed off, away from me. "You're so immature, Phoebe."

"Well, thanks for asking me to paint my nails with you," I called out as she went into her room and shut the door. "Really nice of you to think of me."

I shook my head and told myself to forget about it. After all, I had something more important to worry about. After I went into my room, I shut the door and pulled the box out of my bag. It was so cute. Shiny and silver and, most of all, mysterious.

I had a guess as to who left it there. Sheila had gone around town just as I had, completing the tasks, and she was supposed to leave a gift in the hollow pillar, too. What if it was something valuable? Would I feel guilty about finding it? But of course, if no one else had found it by now, it probably would have sat there for another seventy years.

My hands shook as I unwrapped the bow from the box. And then I slipped the cover off and peered inside.

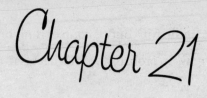

Chapter 21

MULLIGATAWNY: AN ENGLISH SOUP STRONGLY SPICED

WITH CURRY POWDER AND NUTMEG

It was a folded piece of paper. I sat on my bed, opened it, and read what it said.

A poem
written by Sheila Hornbaker

You are my sister,
you are my friend.
Our love and our friendship
are here till the end.

When the sun rises,
I think of you.
When the stars twinkle,
I think of you, too.

There are miles between us
and much to wish for.
But what I wish most of all
is to miss you no more.

I hope you're home soon,
the place you belong.
Our world is so quiet
without your sweet song.

The poem made my chest ache. There was so much missing in so few words. It was incredibly sweet, and I wondered if Kitty had ever seen it. Did Sheila write it a second time and send it to Kitty? Or did the words simply sit in a small hole, in the hopes the gift would help the magic make Sheila's wish come true? Most of all, I wondered, did her wish *ever* come true?

I folded up the letter and put it back in the box, then

stuck it between my mattress and box spring, where I'd also hidden the compact. If Alice decided to ransack my room again, I'd doubt she'd tear my bed apart like some first-rate criminal.

My phone vibrated, so I took it out of my pocket.

Ned: What am I going to do?

Me: About what? Why aren't you sleeping? You need to rest!

Ned: About a gift.

Me: You're going to stop worrying about it right now and rest.

Ned: I should have had you get some tea.

Me: I know!

Ned: Are you going to the cemetery tomorrow?

Me: I'm not sure. Do you want me to get something for your mum from there?

Ned: Like what, an old skull? I don't think she'd like that very much, Phoebe.

Me: Go to sleep.

Ned: Zzzzzzzzz.

I quickly changed my clothes, like I told my mother I'd needed to do, and then, before I had a chance to forget, I wrote this on a yellow index card:

After I stuck it on my bulletin board, I went downstairs.

"Oh, good," Mum said. "Your mulligatawny soup is good and hot. Want some bread and butter to go with it?"

I sat at the table. "Sure. Thanks."

I stirred my soup around as I thought about the last item I needed to complete for the spell.

"Mum?"

"Yes?"

"What do you know about cemeteries in London?"

"You do realize that's a very strange question, don't you?"

I smiled. "I know."

She handed me the small plate of bread before she sat across from me. "May I ask why you want to know?"

"I was thinking I might want to visit one. Do some headstone rubbings with paper and chalk. I've heard of people doing that, and I've always wanted to try it."

"Hm," she said. "Have you ever heard of the Magnificent Seven cemeteries?"

I shook my head as I nibbled on a piece of bread.

"People used to be buried in small churchyards, but those became very crowded, so they established a number of private cemeteries. I believe they were all created in the early 1840s."

"Are the seven all over London, then?" I asked as I pondered how I'd ever figure out which cemetery the spell was referring to, exactly. There was no way I could visit all of them just to be sure I went to the right one. It definitely seemed like I might need to use the Internet to help me with this one.

"Yes," Mum said. "I've only been to a couple of them. If you'd like me to take you to one, I'd be happy to. Tomorrow afternoon might be better, since it's raining now. I work tonight, but could get a little sleep in the morning."

Just then, Alice appeared. "Do you want to go with us?" I asked my sister.

She reached down and took a piece of bread. "Where are you going?"

"Phoebe thought she might like to do some headstone rubbings tomorrow."

"Ew. No thank you." Alice looked at me. "Why in

the world would you want to do that? It's creepy. And immature."

That was the second time in an hour she'd called me immature. And it bothered me. A lot.

"I'm not immature," I quipped back. "Why do you keep saying that?"

She raised her eyebrows. "Maybe because it's true?"

I stood up, tears stinging my eyes. I told myself to keep it together. I couldn't let her see how much she was getting to me. "Fine. I'll go to my room so you don't have to be bothered by my immature self."

"Phoebe," Mum said. "You didn't finish your lunch." She turned to my sister. "Wasn't that a little harsh, Alice? She didn't deserve that."

Alice went to the sink. "All right, all right, I'm sorry."

I really wanted to believe her, but I just didn't.

Chapter 22

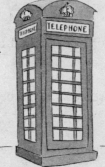

PINCH: TO STEAL

That night, Dad came in to wish me good night. He took my old stuffed teddy, Nicky, off the shelf and sat on my bed.

"You've been awfully quiet since I got home from work," he said. "I'm a bit worried about you."

"Everything I say is wrong," I told him. "So I thought it best that I not say anything at all. It's easier that way."

"Pheebs, that's not true and you know it." He handed Nicky over, and I tucked him in next to me, under my chin. "Mum said you and Alice had a bit of a row this afternoon."

I squeezed Nicky tighter. "I'm so tired of it. Of not getting along with her. What am I supposed to do, Dad?"

"Have you tried talking with her? Sitting down and having a heart-to-heart?"

I sighed. "That'd never work. She doesn't want to talk to me, period."

"But if you told her you really need to let her know how you feel, she might listen."

One thing about my dad? He's always the optimist. Maybe he has to be if he wants to be successful in the antiques business. Every time he goes hunting for new finds, he really believes he'll discover something good. I suppose if he didn't believe that, there'd never be any motivation for him to go out and try.

"I don't know," I said. "I wish she'd just magically change. I want to wake up tomorrow morning and find the old Alice has returned."

He smiled as he rubbed my arm. "It'd certainly be nice if life worked like that, wouldn't it? But I'm sad to tell you, nothing is ever that easy."

If I could get to the cemetery the next day, hopefully it would be that simple. But I didn't tell him that.

"Think about what I said, all right?" Dad said as he stood. "Make a nice pot of tea and some scones, and sit down with her. Let her know how you feel. I'm sure you girls can work things out."

"She'd probably say scones are immature," I mumbled.

He gave me a funny look. "What was that?"

I shook my head. "Nothing. Never mind."

"Good night, Phoebe. Pleasant dreams."

"You too."

After he left, I started to get up and put Nicky back in his spot on the shelf. But I changed my mind. Everything else I'd done that day was immature—might as well keep it up. Besides, he was soft and cuddly. And sometimes, soft and cuddly is just the sort of thing you need to feel better.

The next morning was a different story, however. I did not feel better. In fact, I felt horrible. I woke up early, like six a.m., with a bad stomachache. I tossed and turned for a while, trying to get back to sleep, until I finally got up and went to the kitchen to get a drink of water.

Mum sat at the table eating some toast, still dressed in her scrubs. She'd probably recently gotten home from her shift at the hospital. "You all right, love? It's so early."

"My stomach hurts," I told her.

She came over to me and put her hand to my forehead. "Oh, dear. You feel warm. Let me find the thermometer. Why don't you go back to bed?"

"Can you bring me a glass of water?" I asked. "I'm thirsty."

"Yes. Of course. I'll be there in a minute."

But for the next few hours, I couldn't keep anything down, not even water. Finally, the worst passed and I was able to sleep. When I woke up, I looked at the clock, surprised to see it was already four o'clock in the afternoon. I grabbed my phone off the nightstand and saw I had a few texts.

Ned: Feeling a bit better today, but Mum said I have to rest. Toast has never tasted so good.

Ned: Any new and wonderful ideas for a gift?

Ned: Hello? Hello? Have you been abducted by aliens? Had a terrible pogo stick accident and taken to hospital? I'm worried. Hope you're okay.

Me: Guess who's sick today?

Ned: Oh no! Six lashes with a wet noodle to the poor chap who got you sick.

Me: Not your fault. Hope I'm well enough to come to the party tomorrow.

147

Ned: Me too! It seems to only be a 24-hour thing, so that's good.

My door opened, and Mum peeked her head in. "Oh, you're awake. Feeling better?"

"Yes. I think so. Stomach doesn't hurt, anyway."

"Good. You should drink something. Which sounds better, water or tea?"

"Water, please."

"You got it. I'll be back. Then I need a nap. Been worried about you, so I haven't been able to sleep. I'll ask Alice to check in on you."

"You don't have to do that, Mum. I'll be fine."

She gave me a little smile. Boy, did she look tired. "Hopefully that's true, but it will make me feel better to know she's looking in on you."

I thought about what Dad had said. Maybe when she popped in to make sure I didn't need anything, I could ask her if we could talk. I could try and sound really pitiful, being sick and all, and maybe that would help it go well.

Or, I could pretend to be asleep and not talk to her at all. Decisions, decisions.

Turned out I didn't need to decide what to do because

my horrid sister didn't check on me once, even though Mum had surely asked her to. For all Alice cared, I could have rolled over dead.

I was furious. Dad came home from work and asked if I wanted anything to eat. I told him maybe in another couple of hours I'd try some toast. Then he went back to the kitchen to make something for him and Alice.

While they ate supper together, I pulled the compact out from my mattress and took a picture of it to send to Ned. Because he needed a gift. And Alice didn't deserve the money the compact might fetch. She could stay home and not go to university. It'd serve her right. And as for the cemetery, I decided there was no need. It was hard to imagine there was any magic strong enough to bring the two of us close together again.

So that was that. It was over.

Me: Do you think your mum would like this vintage compact?

Ned. Wow. Where'd you get that?

Me: Paris.

Ned: It looks expensive. Did you pinch it from someone?

Me: No. I'm just very good at bartering.

Ned: Doesn't your dad want to sell it at the shop?

Me: I'm the one who found it. I figure I can do what I want with it. So if you think your mum would like it, you can have it.

Ned: Thanks, Phoebe! I think she'll love it. So you'll bring it to the party?

Me: Yes. See you then.

The next day, I put on my robe and ventured out of my room, because I was actually hungry. Dad had gone into work and Alice was still sleeping. Mum had the next few days off, and was about to mop the kitchen floor.

"Oh, Phoebe, you look much better. You've got some color in your cheeks again. You hungry?"

"Is Prince Harry completely adorable?" I replied as I sat at the table.

She laughed. "I'll take that as a yes. Let's start with some applesauce and see how that goes down. If all goes well, you can have some porridge if you'd like."

While she got the bowl and spoon, I asked, "What time shall we leave for the party?"

She turned around. "Sweetheart, I'm afraid you'll have to miss it. It's too soon for you to get out and about."

"But I feel so much better. Really and truly. I slept most of the day yesterday, and all night, too. As long as I keep eating, I'm sure I'll be fine. Ned is counting on me to be there."

She set the bowl of applesauce in front of me. "I'm sure he'll be disappointed if you can't make it, but we simply cannot jeopardize your health for a silly party."

I could feel my cheeks getting warm. "It's not a silly party! It's going to be special, and we should all be there."

"I'm sorry, I didn't mean it like that. I meant that it's not something important, like school. I know you'll be sad to miss it, but I think it's for the best. We wouldn't want you to do too much too soon and end up back in bed."

I shoveled the applesauce into my mouth, all the while trying to figure out how to change her mind. There had to be a way. There just had to be.

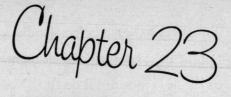

Chapter 23

RUBBISH: NONSENSE

After I ate both my applesauce and porridge, I went back to my room. The thermometer was still on my nightstand, so I took my temperature. After it beeped, I stuck my head out into the hallway and yelled, "Mum, my temperature is perfectly normal. Just thought you should know."

"Happy to hear it!" she called back. "Now back to bed, and take it easy."

But I didn't want to take it easy. I wanted to shower and get rid of my greasy bed-head hair. Besides, if I looked a hundred percent normal, how could she refuse me when I asked her again later if she'd allow me to go to the party?

So I rounded up my clothes and went to the loo. But the door was locked. I stood and waited. A few minutes later, Alice appeared. I hadn't seen her in more than twenty-four hours, something she was probably absolutely thrilled about.

"Feeling better, I hope?" she asked me.

"Like you care," I muttered as I slipped past her.

"Wait," she said, gently grabbing my wrist. I turned to face her. "Why do you say that? I really meant it. I *do* hope you're feeling better. Being ill is the worst, especially while on school holiday." I didn't say anything. She slid her hand down and gave my hand a tiny squeeze before she let go. "I'm sorry about the way I've acted lately, Phoebe. I know I haven't been myself. Paris was so wonderful, and I wish it could be that way always."

"What do you mean?"

"You know, wandering around, eating good food, meeting interesting people—with no responsibility, really. I mean, yes, we were looking for antiques, sort of, but it wasn't work. Not really."

It was like she was opening a door for me. Not a bathroom door, but a door to a conversation. My sister was talking to me, finally, and I knew I needed to walk through and see where the doorway led us. It seemed like it should be easy, taking the first step. After all, I'd talked to lots of strangers this past week. But when it's someone you love, it's harder for some reason. Maybe because if they slam the door in your face, it will hurt. A lot.

I leaned up against the bathroom doorjamb and took a deep breath. "Alice, what's going on? I mean, really going on? Aren't you excited about university anymore?"

She sighed as she ran her fingers through her hair. Then she leaned in and whispered, "Dad keeps going on and on about the added expenses, and I can't help but feel guilty. This week, it's really started to sink in what it all means, and honestly? I'm scared to death."

"But that's rubbish. You've wanted to go to medical school for as long as I can remember."

"I know! But what if I can't do it? What if Mum and Dad spend their hard-earned money to get me there, and I fail?"

"You are not going to fail."

"You don't know that."

"Actually, I do."

"How? Can you magically see the future somehow?"

"Yes. I can. And what I see is the determined girl I've known my entire life who works hard and makes things happen. You will do fine, Alice. Really. Now, may I go and take my shower please?"

She looked at me for a second, her eyes soft and kind. I swear she almost appeared . . . grateful. Did I finally say the right thing for once? Of course, I knew she'd never tell me so. But I took some pleasure in that expression she wore for one brief moment.

"Shower away," she said. "But not too long. We don't want you fainting from exhaustion or something equally horrible."

She left and closed the door behind her. As I undressed, I recalled what Dad had said about having a heart-to-heart talk with Alice. Is that what we'd just done? It wasn't as special as it might have been over tea and scones, but it seemed to me that something had shifted between us. She'd confided in me about how she was feeling, and I'd reassured her that she would do what she needed to do and everything would be all right. And the surprising thing? I really meant it.

As I stepped into the shower, I suddenly realized one awful thing, though. I'd given away the compact that could have provided some much-needed money for her university education. I couldn't ever let her know that.

Ever.

Chapter 24

SHEARS: SCISSORS

At lunch, I ate not one, but two bowls of soup. "You *are* feeling better," my mother exclaimed.

"I told you," I said. "May I please go to the party? Please?"

"She seems fine, Mum," Alice said. "I think you should let her go."

I could hardly believe my sister was standing up for me. It made me wish I'd had that heart-to-heart with her much sooner. It also made me feel even guiltier about the compact. But I couldn't think about that. It was done, and there wasn't anything I could do about it now.

"Rest up this afternoon, and if you still feel fine after teatime, I suppose you may go," Mum said.

A nap was a small price to pay, so I agreed. Except, I ended up sleeping much longer than I'd planned, and so I was discombobulated when I woke up. There'd be no teatime for me. I quickly changed into a blue dress I'd chosen for the occasion and then started gathering my things. I realized I'd been so focused on Ned's gift for his mum that I hadn't prepared anything for her. So I quickly made her a card with some colored pencils and hoped Mum and Dad would sign all of our names to whatever gift they'd be giving her.

"Phoebe," Dad called from the hallway. "We need to get a move on or we're going to be late."

"Coming!" I yelled.

From my window I could see that it wasn't raining, so I grabbed my white cardigan sweater, my bag, the card for Mrs. Chapman, the compact in its little black pouch, and my phone. I rushed out my bedroom door, trying to get my bag open so I could shove everything inside, and ran smack-dab into my father, causing me to drop everything I'd been holding.

"What's taking so long?" Alice asked as she walked toward us.

Dad crouched down to help me, and though the first thing I went for was the black pouch, he reached it first.

"What's this?" Dad asked, standing up and eyeing it suspiciously.

"What's what?" Alice asked.

Oh no, I thought to myself. This was not good.

"It's a gift," I said. "For Ned's mum. May I have it back, please?"

But of course he couldn't return it to me without opening the pouch first. His eyes lit up when he saw what it was.

"Phoebe!" he exclaimed. "Where'd you get this?"

Alice peered over his arm. "What is it, Dad?"

"It's a vintage Cartier compact," he replied as he turned it over in his hands, and then opened it up to take a peek on the inside. I'd taken the letter and photograph out because I wanted to keep those for myself. "It's in excellent condition." He looked at me. "Where did you find this?"

There was no way out that I could see. I had to tell them the truth, and they'd just have to accept the fact that I'd decided to give it away. I'd found it, so it seemed to me I shouldn't feel badly about doing with it what I pleased.

"Paris," I said. "At the flea market. I got it for a steal. Ned needed a gift for his mother, so I told him he could have it."

My sister's mouth practically dropped to the floor. "You're giving it to *Ned*? Phoebe, have you lost your mind? Surely it's worth a lot of money. How could you do that? Cartier is the brand we always watch for, you and I, when we're antiques hunting together. You had to have known it was valuable."

"I . . . I wasn't quite sure. And besides, you were being so mean to me all the time. So I just . . ."

"So you just decided you'd throw away a small fortune that could have been used for my university expenses?" Alice shook her head before she headed toward her room. "I cannot believe you would do something like this to me."

"Alice," I said. "What I haven't told you yet is what was inside the compact. It was a letter with a magical spell designed to bring two people close together again. I've been doing the items in the spell all week, so you and I could be close again. So believe what you want, but I didn't do this to make you angry with me. Really, it's the last thing I want."

Alice scoffed. "A magical spell? Because you want to get close to me? Well, here's an idea—tell me when you find something fabulous at a Paris flea market. Don't you think I would have been excited with you? But now you've given it away and ruined everything."

The way she said the last bit, it was like she'd taken a pair of shears and cut my heart in half.

As my sister turned to leave, Dad said, "Alice, come along, now. Let's go to the car. Hopefully we can sort all of this out."

"I don't want to, Dad," Alice said. "Go on to the party without me. I'm suddenly ill. I'm sure they'll understand when you explain I've come down with the nasty virus Ned and Phoebe had."

After she shut her door, Dad helped me gather the rest of my things. He didn't say a word as we walked toward the front door together.

Mum stood there looking at her phone. "Is everything all right? Sounded like Alice was upset."

"She's upset, that's for sure," Dad replied.

"Where is she?" Mum asked. "Oh no. She's not going with us?"

"No. It's fine, Collette. She can stay home. She said to tell the Chapmans she's not feeling well."

Mum looked at me. "What in the world happened this time?"

"Let's go," Dad said. "I'll explain on the way."

While he drove across town, Dad explained what had happened. He left out the part about the letter, which I was thankful for. Mum would not have been happy if she'd learned I'd been lying about what I was doing in London. He probably didn't want to upset her before the party.

"What are we going to do?" she asked when he'd finished with the story.

"I don't suppose there's anything we can do," Dad replied. "Phoebe has promised the compact to Ned, and I think we need to honor that promise."

"I disagree," Mum said. "I think she should talk to him about it. She could ask him if she can keep the compact after all. He might be understanding."

I thought back to all the horrible things Alice had said to me in the hallway. "I don't want to do that, though," I said. "Like Dad said, I promised it to Ned, and so, I'm going to give it to Ned. I'm the one who found it, so seems to me I should have the final say as to what happens to it."

"I wish you'd shown it to me earlier, Phoebe," Dad said.

"I was going to surprise you and Alice with it," I said softly as I looked out the window. "But then I decided Alice didn't deserve it, really. And Ned had been so nice to me all week . . ."

"Well, I hope his mum knows what a special thing she's getting," my mother said.

It felt like the right thing, giving the compact to Ned like we'd discussed. And yet, at the same time, it also felt very, very wrong. It was a strange, mixed-up feeling, and I didn't like it one bit.

Chapter 25

DISHY: GOOD-LOOKING

When we got to the restaurant, a sign with CHAPMAN PARTY and an arrow pointing upstairs showed us the way.

"Think they reserved the entire second floor?" Dad asked Mum as we made our way up the stairs.

"Most likely," Mum replied. "Makes it extra special that way." She turned to me. "Feeling all right, Phoebe?"

"Yes," I said. "I'm fine." I glanced at the small gift she carried. "What did you get her?"

"A lovely bottle of perfume," Mum said. "Chanel No. 5. It's not something women splurge on for themselves, but it's nice to receive as a gift."

163

"Did you sign my name on the card?" I asked.

"Yes, it's from all of us."

"I made her a card at home, but do you think that's immature?" Clearly, my sister had given me a complex.

"Phoebe, it's not immature; it's thoughtful," Dad said. "She'll be thrilled you went to the trouble to do that for her."

Upstairs, groups of people were standing around and mingling, while others were seated on sofas or stools. It was a relaxed environment, not formal and stuffy, and I was glad about that.

We hadn't made it far when a waiter approached us and asked if we'd like something to drink. My dad ordered three ginger ales for us, which sounded really good to me. I searched the room for Ned, and when I found him, talking to Chester, he waved me over. I put my finger up to tell him it'd be just a moment. I wanted to get my drink first. The waiter returned a minute later with our order. I asked my parents, "Can I go see Ned? I need to give him the compact."

"You're absolutely sure that's what you want to do?" Dad asked.

"Yes," I said.

"All right," Mum said. "We're going to find the birthday girl and extend our best wishes. We'll come find you later."

When I reached Ned and Chester, Chester said, "Hello, Phoebe."

"Hello." Both of them were dressed up in jackets and ties. I thought Chester looked especially handsome. The light blue shirt he wore looked really good with his blond hair and deep blue eyes. "The two of you are looking quite dishy, I must say."

Chester's cheeks turned pink. Ned proudly stuck his chest out, or tried to anyway. He's so skinny it's not like there's much to stick out. "We do, don't we?"

"Never mind," I said with a smile. "I take it back. Your head doesn't need to get any bigger than it already is."

He nudged me with his elbow. "You love my big head and you know it. And I'm so glad you're here! I was starting to worry you might have been too ill to come. Hadn't heard from you today."

"If Mum had her way, I'd be at home in bed. But I somehow managed to convince her I'd be fine." I leaned in closer. "Still, would it be all right if we found some seats?"

They both turned and looked behind them. "There's three chairs," Chester said. "Back in the corner. Let's grab them."

After we took a seat, Ned asked, "So. Can I see it? Mum's gift?"

I took a big sip of my drink, then set it on the floor by my chair so I could get the pouch out of my bag. "I'm sorry I didn't have time to wrap it."

He opened the pouch and let the compact fall into his palm. "Whoa. It's even more amazing in person."

"Is it old?" Chester asked as he peered over Ned's arm.

"Yes. From the nineteen-thirties or so," I said. "Remember the photo and letter I told you about, Ned? This is where I found them. They were tucked inside of it. I believe this compact belonged to Kitty, who received the letter and photo from her sister."

Ned's eyes got big and round. "This belonged to *Kitty*?"

"Who's Kitty?" Chester asked as he loosened his tie a bit.

Before I could say anything, Ned jumped in and explained about the letter Sheila wrote to Kitty and the magical spell and how we'd been visiting the places mentioned in the letter, just like Sheila had done. He got through it much more quickly than I would have, which was probably a good thing.

"She has one more place to go and then the spell is complete," Ned replied. He turned and looked at me. "Right?"

"Yes. We were going to go yesterday, but then I got sick. Although I have no idea which cemetery is the correct one. My mother said there's seven around London, and there's no way I can talk her into going to all of them."

Chester hadn't stopped staring at the compact. I could tell there was something he was trying to sort out.

"Does the idea of a magic spell bother you, Chester?" I asked him.

"No. I'm just curious why you're giving away the compact. It has so much history." His blue eyes were warm and kind. He seemed to truly be concerned. "Don't you want to keep it?"

Before I could answer, Ned jumped in again. "Of course she doesn't. She wants my mum to have it. She knows it will be well taken care of. Besides, she still has the photo and the letter—those are the important items, right, Pheebs?"

I swallowed hard and did my best to smile. "Yes. Absolutely."

But it was like Chester could see right through me. Now that I was here, thinking about Sheila and Kitty all over again, and wishing and hoping the two sisters had been reunited back in 1941, I couldn't ignore the niggling feeling any longer.

I shouldn't have promised the compact to Ned.

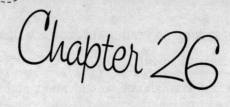

Chapter 26

KNACKERED: TIRED

Mrs. Chapman seemed shocked by the vintage Cartier makeup compact. I think she liked it, but it was sort of hard to tell. "Where in the world did you find this, Ned?" she asked him.

"It's a secret," he replied, looking like a cat that had just swallowed a canary. "It doesn't really matter, does it? As long as you love it, that's the important thing."

"Well, thank you, dear," she said. And then she went on and opened another gift. After her birthday presents were all opened, a band came out and some of the adults danced. Ned, Chester, and I continued to sit in the corner talking and eating snacks the waiters brought by every once in a while.

When I got home, I said good night to my parents and went to my room. I knew something was up when I saw the light on. I found Alice waiting for me at my desk.

"What are you doing in here?" I asked.

"Did you have fun at the party?" she asked without looking at me.

"It was all right."

"Did Ned's mother like her gift?"

"That's a silly question. Of course she did. Her son gave it to her. She would have liked anything he gave her."

Now she looked at me. And what a look it was—her eyes narrow and her lips pinched tightly together. "Exactly! Which is why you never should have given away that valuable antique. I mean, really, Phoebe. Do I not mean anything to you?"

It felt like she might never stop beating me up about this. "Alice, I found the thing. Do you not get that? It was *mine*, to do with as I pleased."

"No," she said, her face red. "Dad sent us out to find

antiques for *him*. You used *his* money to buy the compact. It wasn't yours to give away!"

I sat on my bed in a huff. "But I did give it away, and there's nothing we can do about it now. It's done and over with. So please, I'm knackered and I'd like to go to bed now."

As she stared at me, probably trying to figure out if she should give up the fight, I wondered how things had gotten even worse than before. For a moment yesterday, it seemed like things were better. Like we'd made it past the worst of whatever we were going through. But now, it was hard to imagine ever getting along with her.

I felt so sad about it all—like I'd lost something very, very special. Something even more special than a vintage Cartier piece. And that's when I realized perhaps I was the one who needed to give up the fight.

"I'm sorry, Alice," I said softly. "I don't know what else to say. But I truly am sorry. You're right, I suppose. I shouldn't have given it away."

She didn't say anything, just let out a deep sigh before she turned around and left, closing the door behind her.

I really was exhausted and I knew the best thing to do was to wash my face, brush my teeth, and get ready for bed. But I didn't move. Instead, I stared at the bulletin board, recalling my little adventures around London with Ned. Had Sheila felt defeated at any point? Did she hit any road bumps along the way? *If only I could talk to her*, I thought. I needed to know if the magic had worked. Because if it did, then I wouldn't stop. I would somehow figure out how to visit all seven cemeteries, if that's what it would take to get close to my sister again.

And that's when it hit me. An idea. A *big* idea. I quietly opened my door and peered down the hallway. It was dark and quiet. It seemed Mum and Dad had gone to their room, which meant it was a fine time to use the computer in Dad's study. Hopefully, Alice had gone to bed as well. I'd need to be quiet, just in case.

After I tiptoed down the hall to the study, I opened the door slowly, hoping it wouldn't creak. It didn't. Once inside, I shut the door, flipped on the light, and scurried to the computer. Fortunately for me, Dad hadn't powered it off, so it was only in sleep mode.

Thanks to the poem I found, I now knew Sheila's full name. I opened the Internet browser and typed "Sheila Hornbaker" into the search engine box. The first few results didn't seem to be anything helpful. But at the bottom of the page was something quite interesting. I clicked on the link and found a short article, dated a year ago, in the *Blackheath Bugle*.

"Sheila Hornbaker, a resident of Blackheath, has made a large donation toward the Manor House Gardens . . ."

I didn't need to read further. I had exactly what I needed. As of a year ago, Sheila was alive, and she lived in a neighboring borough. I might actually be able to go and visit her!

Chapter 27

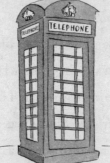

BLATANT: OBVIOUS

The next morning, I woke up and went to the kitchen to make some muffins. The house was quiet. Peaceful. As I dumped the various ingredients into the mixing bowl, I remembered the times Alice had stood next to me, teaching me the correct way to measure the flour or to stir the batter so it didn't get overmixed. Now, following each step and doing it the "right" way was almost second nature to me. She'd taught me well. I hoped she knew that.

Dad was up shortly after me since Saturday is often the busiest day at the shop.

"What are you making?" he asked as he peeked in the bowl.

"Banana nut muffins."

"Is there a special occasion I'm not aware of?"

"No. I'm just trying to butter you up," I replied.

He chuckled. "Ah, the old banana nut muffin butter-up trick. That's a good one, Pheebs. Clever girl."

I scooped the batter into the muffin cups and then popped the pan into the oven. Dad put the kettle on for some tea.

"Go on then, tell me what's on your mind," he said as he took a seat at the table.

"You don't want to wait for your breakfast?"

"I'll probably take a couple with me. Need to get to work early this morning. Lots to do."

I nodded. "All right, then. I have a favor to ask you."

"I figured it was something like that."

"I think Sheila, or Ms. Hornbaker as I should probably call her, the woman who wrote the letter I found in the makeup compact, is still alive, and I'd like to try and find her. I'd love to meet her and return the photograph and letter to her. And I have some questions for her—about the magic spell and her sister, Kitty."

"How do you know she's still alive?" he asked.

"I found her. On the Internet. As of a year ago, she was living in Blackheath. Can you believe that, Dad? She's *so* close to us! I'm hoping she hasn't moved since then, and you can help me track down her address."

Dad stared at me. He truly seemed to be gobsmacked by this news. "You really want to go and see her?"

"Yes. It's hard to explain, but I feel a sort of connection to her. Like I know her, but I don't. And I want to *really* get to know her, at least a little bit. Does that make sense?"

"Hm. I'm not sure I really understand the pull you feel, but I suppose there's no harm in visiting her. If we can find her, that is. Although I'm not going to take you until you tell your mother about the photograph and the letter you found. I saved that bit for you to share with her."

"Thanks a lot, Dad," I said sarcastically.

He smiled. "No problem."

When the timer went off, I pulled the muffins out of the oven. Dad put some tea in a thermos, grabbed a couple of muffins, and was on his way. It wasn't long before he rang me from the shop's phone.

"I think I've found Sheila's address," he told me. I

could hear him tapping on his computer keys. "When would you like to go see her?"

"Can we go today?" I asked. "Please? When you get home from work?"

"You certainly are eager, aren't you? I suppose that will be as good a time as any. Make sure you let your mother know what's happening before I get home."

"I will. Bye, Dad."

"Good-bye."

It was a while later when Mum woke up. After I'd showered and dressed, I'd placed the photo and the letter at her spot at the table, along with a cup of tea and a plate of muffins.

"What's this?" she asked as she picked up the photograph.

"That was inside the compact I got in Paris," I said. "Along with the letter that's there as well. I'd like you to read it, please."

She carefully unfolded the piece of stationary and quietly took in the words. When she finished, she looked up at me. "Her sister was sent away during the war. Can you imagine what that must have been like for her parents? For all of them, really?"

"No," I said as I sat at the table next to her. "I can't. It must have been so hard. On everyone." I swallowed. "I actually have a confession to make. When Ned and I went into London, we weren't only looking for a birthday gift. I was also visiting the places in the letter."

She gave me a funny look. "You were? But why?"

I took a deep breath. "Because I wanted some of that magic to work on me and *my* sister. I want to be close with her again, Mum. And I thought if it worked for Sheila and Kitty, it might work for me and Alice, too."

"So you lied to me?" she asked, disappointment replacing the confusion.

"Not really," I said quietly. "I just didn't tell you the entire truth."

"In my eyes, that's still lying. I'm not happy about this, Phoebe. You should have told me what you were doing. All of it."

"But you might not have let me go," I said. "And I really wanted the magic to work. Like, you don't know how badly."

She glanced at the letter again. "So *this* is why you wanted to go to the cemetery."

I nodded. "Yes. It's the only place I haven't visited."

"Is that why you're showing this to me now? So I'll take you to the cemetery?"

"Actually, no. Last night I decided I wanted to see if I could find Sheila. And I did! She lives nearby, in Blackheath. And Dad said we could visit her later today, but only if I told you about the letter."

"I see," she said. "Well, I hope you'll understand that I can't, in good conscience, let you go to the cemetery now."

I hadn't expected this. I knew she might be upset with me, but to keep me from completing the spell? How could she do that to me, when I was *so* close?

"But, Mum—"

She didn't let me finish. "I'm sure you're disappointed, but my decision is final. There has to be some consequences to your actions, after all. Besides, in my opinion, there are much better ways to get close to your sister. Excuse the blatant suggestion, but have you tried talking to her?"

"That's what Dad suggested, too."

"Brilliant. I'm happy to hear that we're on the same page. Does that mean you'll give it a go?"

"I already did, and she's still not happy with me." I paused as I thought about how everything went down.

"Well, things might have been all right for a little while, but then she found out about the compact and that ruined everything. I'm pretty sure at this point, the only thing that's going to help us is some good old-fashioned magic."

Mum took a bite of her muffin. "These are good, Phoebe."

"Thanks."

"Did you use any magic to make them?" she asked.

"What? No. Of course not. I carefully followed a recipe, and did everything that needed to be done."

"Hm. Interesting," she said. "Sometimes doing what needs to be done makes all the difference, doesn't it?"

She was trying to make a point. And just the thought of trying to make things right when it came to the compact gave me a stomachache. But I knew something needed to be done. And fast.

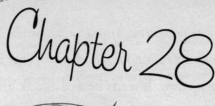

Chapter 28

FANCY: LIKE

I went to my room and rang Ned. He was probably sleeping, but I couldn't wait. I needed to get the difficult conversation over with.

It took a long time, but he finally answered. "Hello?" he said in a very sleepy voice.

"Ned, I know it's early and I probably woke you, and I'm sorry. But this is important. Are you listening? Like, are you completely awake?"

"Hm?"

"Go splash some cold water on your face."

"What? No. I don't want to. What time is it, anyway?"

"It's almost nine. In two days you'll have to get up early and go to school, you know. This is for the best, waking up now. It won't be as difficult on Monday."

"That's rubbish," he said. "It's going to be very difficult on Monday. So I fancy as much sleep as I can get today, thank you very much."

"But this is important, Ned."

"Yes. You already told me that." He grumbled a bit before he said, "All right. I'm sitting up and completely awake. Happy now?"

"Good. Thank you. Please know this is not easy, but I have to do it."

"Do what?"

I gulped hard. "I have to ask you to return the makeup compact. I wasn't supposed to give it you."

"What do you mean? You said you found it in Paris, so wasn't it yours to do with as you pleased?"

"Well . . . not really. I bought it with Dad's money. And I was there looking for vintage items because he asked me to do that. And because we were hoping to find some valuable items we might sell to help with some of Alice's university costs. She'll get scholarships, of course. But having to travel back and forth between London and America is expensive, and—"

He didn't let me finish. "So you should have given it to him." It was a statement, not a question.

"Yes. I got caught up in the magic spell and the letter, so I didn't tell them about it right away. And then I got angry with Alice and offered it to you. I'm sorry, Ned. Do you think if we explain the situation to your mum, she'll understand?"

"Actually, we don't have to do that. We're coming over later to give it back to you."

I sat up straight and tall. "What?"

"She knew it must be valuable. And she wouldn't stop bothering me until I told her where I got it. When I told her you gave it to me, she insisted that we return it to its rightful owners. In other words, she knew you'd made a mistake giving it away like you did."

"Ned," I said, a bit annoyed, "why didn't you say that five minutes ago?"

"I don't know. Maybe I wanted to see you grovel. Such a funny word, isn't it?"

"Grovel? Like, beg, you mean?"

"Yes. For my understanding. And forgiveness."

I laughed. I couldn't help it! "Ned, you're mean. Am I supposed to be honored to have your forgiveness?"

"Absolutely! It was quite annoying to have to find another gift to give my mother."

"What'd you come up with?"

"I drew her a picture of her favorite bird, which is the Eurasian jay. It has brilliant turquoise feathers. And you'll be happy to know, it turned out splendidly."

"See? Everything has sorted itself, then. Alice will get some money for university, I get to meet Sheila Hornbaker, and your mum gets a lovely gift from her son. Well, I suppose I should say, *almost* everything is sorted. Alice and I still aren't getting along."

"Wait. Phoebe, did you say you get to meet Sheila?"

"Oh, right. I was so busy groveling I forgot to tell you that bit of good news. Dad thinks he's found her address, and when he gets home from the shop, we're going to visit her. Can you believe it? I might actually find out whether or not the magic spell worked. Because right now, it feels like it may be my only hope with my sister. Things have gone from bad to worse with the two of us."

"I'll wish you lots of luck, then. But Pheebs?"

"Yes?"

"May I please go back to sleep now?"

I laughed. "Only if you promise to bring the compact over before lunchtime. I want to have it here when Dad comes home."

"Can I stay for lunch?" he asked.

"Probably not," I said. "But I made banana muffins. Want to take home a few of those?"

"Can't you bring them over now? They'd make a great breakfast."

"Nope. See you when you get here."

"Fine. Good-bye."

After we said our farewells, I grabbed a pink note-card and wrote the following:

I made a mistake, but it's not the end of the world. I suppose it hardly ever is.

After I pinned it to my bulletin board, I went down the hall to Alice's room. She was probably still sleeping. She would probably *not* be happy if I woke her up. But I didn't want to wait. I wanted to tell her the good news. So much had happened since she'd become upset with me last night before the party.

So I knocked quietly. No response. I knocked louder.

Still not a word from Alice. I swear the girl could sleep through a fire alarm. I opened the door and went over to her bed. She had the pillow practically wrapped around her head. No wonder she couldn't hear the knocking.

I gently, carefully, placed my hand on her back, which was facing me, since she was curled up in a ball, and shook her slightly as I said, "Alice? Hello?"

She sat straight up, her eyes wide with terror. "What is it? What's going on?"

"I need to talk to you."

If eyes could shoot daggers, hers would have shot to kill. She didn't say a single word. Instead, she threw herself down on the bed, face first, with a loud moan. Before I could say anything else, she grabbed the pillow and covered her head with it again. The message was loud and clear—scram.

It seemed like there was nothing else to do but wait for her to wake up in her own time. And hope I hadn't done yet one more thing to make her want to never speak to me again.

Chapter 29

HOLIDAY: VACATION

The day was long and boring. Mum had Alice and I do chores, which is an absolutely horrid way to spend one of the last days of school holiday. To make matters worse, Ned texted me to tell me they couldn't come over until later in the evening because their car had a flat tire that needed to be fixed.

Meanwhile, every time I tried to talk to Alice, she wouldn't have any of it. Pretty soon I decided I didn't want to tell her the good news, because she didn't *deserve* anything good. Mum told me to leave her alone and give her some time to cool off, so that's what I did.

Dad came home a bit earlier than usual, which cheered me right up. "Ready to go?" he asked me as I put away the last of the clean dishes.

"I can't wait! Let me just grab my things."

"I'll tell Alice to get ready as well," Mum said.

I looked at her. "Wait. Are we all going?"

"Yes. I think this will be a rather interesting meeting, and I would love for all of us to be there."

I turned to Dad. "I want you to know I called Ned and asked if we could have the compact back. He said he and his mother had already discussed it and had decided that was the best thing to do, because of its value."

He smiled. "Pheebs, that's wonderful! I'm so proud of you. Have you told Alice the news yet?"

"I tried. It's a long story. But in a way, I think maybe it's best that I haven't. Because all day I've been thinking about meeting Sheila—imagining me showing her the letter and photo I found. How can I possibly do that without giving her the compact as well? I mean, it must have belonged to her sister, right? And I think it would be terrible of us to keep it, when it may have been one of her sister's most treasured things."

No one said anything for a moment. Finally, my mother said, "I think she has a point, Peter."

My dad turned to my mum. "I finally made time today to do a fair amount of research. The compact is worth more than I even imagined. Trips back and forth between here and America during holidays will be paid for. And not just the first year, but most likely *all four years*."

Mum and I both let out a little gasp.

"Dad. Are you serious?"

He walked over to me and put his arm around me. "Yes. Completely. Sweetheart, I know you have a good heart, and because of that, you want to do the right thing. But I don't see how we can possibly give it back when we could really use the money."

Suddenly, this whole thing seemed messy and ugly, and I wished I had three of the compacts, so there was enough to go around. But of course that was impossible. There was only one, and obviously Dad felt very strongly it was now his to do with as he pleased.

"I don't see how I can go and visit this kind, old lady and tell her I found the compact and not give it to her. That will seem so selfish."

"I can see your point," Mum said. "But I also under-stand what your father is saying. We bought the compact fair and square, so it's ours to do with as we please."

"Perhaps," Dad said, "there is a solution here we're not thinking of."

"Which is?" I asked.

"I wonder if it might be best if you didn't go and meet Ms. Hornbaker after all. If it's going to make you feel badly about the entire situation, there's no one say-ing you *have* to go."

Not go? How could he even suggest that? I wanted to meet the woman behind the letter, and to find out what had happened to Kitty. I wanted to know if the spell worked, and if it did, if she had any tips for me as I tried to complete it. Why, she might even know which of the seven cemeteries the spell was talking about.

"Dad, I have to go," I said, trying not to sound like a whiny brat. "It's important to me. I can't even describe how important it is. All I know is I *have* to meet her."

"Then you have to figure out how to tell her that we're keeping the compact," Dad said. "Because you can't give it back to her. You simply can't. We need it too much."

Chapter 30

BLINDING: AWESOME

I grabbed my things while Mum went and told Alice where we were going. I didn't know what I'd say to Ms. Hornbaker about the compact, but I knew that not going altogether was not an option. So we were going. And I'd have to figure out what to say on the way. Or when it came up, at the very latest. Maybe she'd hate me for it, but maybe not. Maybe she'd understand. I could only hope.

"I don't really see why I have to go along with you," Alice said as she slid into the backseat next to me. I repressed a groan. Of course she had to be bratty right off the bat. "Is this why you woke me earlier?" she asked me. "To tell me about this?"

"Maybe," I said. She was still being horrible. So for now, the good news about keeping the compact was staying with me. It was as if she was dead keen on being in a bad mood. I mean, she was acting as if we was taking her to scrub the streets of London with a toothbrush. As I imagined that, I kind of wished it was true. I'd suggest a certain lamppost near a shoe shop and an Indian restaurant to start with. Wouldn't she enjoy that?

"I think it'll be good for you," Dad said as he pulled out onto the road. "Meeting other people and hearing about their hardships can often be an eye-opening experience."

"It can make you feel grateful for all the things you take for granted," Mum explained.

"Are you saying I'm ungrateful?" Alice asked. "Thanks a lot, Mum."

"I didn't mean it that way," Mum said. "Besides, I think we all need a reminder from time to time, no matter who we are."

That's not what I would have said. I would have said, "The truth hurts, so deal with it." But I bit my tongue and kept my thoughts to myself.

Dad turned on the radio, and that was the end of the conversation, thank goodness. I didn't want to listen to any more of Alice's complaining.

When we reached the little white house, Dad parked on the street and turned the engine off. I sat there for a moment, my heart beating like I'd just finished a race. I was nervous. Or excited. Probably both.

"You ready, lovey?" Mum asked.

"I don't know, but I suppose we're about to find out," I replied.

I thought of Nora in Paris, and how she'd had to go to all of those places and talk to complete strangers about her beloved grandmother. It hadn't always been easy for her, but she'd done it. And in the end, the treasure hunt had been a blinding success, all because she didn't let a bit of fear stop her. I carried Nora's strength up the stairs to the porch and gave a quick, loud knock.

And then we waited. And waited. I finally turned around and looked at Mum and Dad, disappointment filling me up like air in a balloon. "I don't think she's home."

But before they could respond, the door slowly creaked open.

"Hello?" the elderly lady said. She was tall and thin and had a bit of a bump at the top of her back. She walked slightly bent over, as if her spine wouldn't straighten out all the way anymore. "How may I help you?"

"Hello," I said. "Are you by chance Sheila Hornbaker?"

"That I am. And who are you?"

I gulped. We'd really found her! "My name is Phoebe Ainsworth. And this is my family: my dad, Peter; my mum, Collette; and my older sister, Alice. We've come because I wanted to meet you after I read a letter you wrote to your sister, Kitty, during World War Two."

At the mention of the word *Kitty*, her eyebrows shot up.

"A letter?" she asked. "To Kitty? Well, how utterly fascinating." She opened the door completely. "Please, won't you come in?"

"You don't mind?" I asked.

"No, not at all. I'll put the kettle on for some tea and then we can chat. How does that sound?"

"Perfect, thank you," I responded.

She led us into the front room of her house, which was filled with beautiful vintage furniture. I looked over at Dad, knowing he'd be eyeing it all with interest. And envy. He ran his hand down the back of a gold loveseat that was lined with ornately carved wood and tufted cushions. He and my sister took a seat together, while Mum and I sat on a larger sofa—a red one, also with tufted cushions.

When Ms. Hornbaker came back to join us, Dad told her, "These are some beautiful French provincial pieces you have, Ms. Hornbaker."

"Please, call me Sheila," she replied. "That goes for all of you. And thank you. I've gathered quite the collection over the years. I tell myself I have enough, and then I find a new piece I adore, and before I know what I've done, I've made another purchase."

"My dad runs an antiques shop," I told her.

She smiled. "Brilliant. I'll have to make a visit. If it's not too far?"

"Not far at all," Dad said. "Greenwich."

While Dad had been admiring the furniture, I'd been eyeing an old black-and-white photo on the mantle. "That photo up there," I said, pointing. "In the pretty red frame. Is that you and Kitty?"

"It is, indeed," Sheila replied. She took a seat while I

went over to take a closer look. "It was taken right before she was sent off to live with her host family."

I stared at the girls in the photo, so happy to finally know what both of them looked like in real life. The strange thing was, they didn't look that different from what I'd imagined in my head. Of course, I'd had the picture of Sheila, but nothing to tell me what Kitty had looked like.

"So please, do tell me," Sheila said, "how did you come to find one of my letters to Kitty?"

And here it was, the question I'd been dreading. I didn't even get a chance to ask her any of my questions first. Still, it didn't seem like there was anything to do but answer her. I took a deep breath and hoped this nice lady with beautiful furniture would continue to be nice when she heard what I was about to tell her.

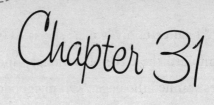

Chapter 31

BITS AND BOBS: VARIOUS THINGS

When we were in Paris last week," I began as I returned to the sofa to sit down, "I stumbled upon a booth at a flea market with lots of bits and bobs. Straight away, I was attracted to a vintage makeup compact, which I purchased for a small sum. It must have belonged to your sister, because inside I found a black-and-white photo of you along with a letter you wrote to her." I reached into my bag, pulled the items out, and handed them to her.

A pair of reading glasses hung from a chain around her neck, and so she put them on and peered at the photo. "That certainly is me," she said. Next, she carefully unfolded the piece of stationary and I watched as her eyes scanned the page. "Oh my goodness," she said. "The magical spell! I'd forgotten all about this."

Forgotten? How in the world could she have forgotten about something like that? Unless . . .

"Did it work?" I asked, probably a little too eagerly. "Did it bring your sister home to you? I've been dying to know ever since I found it."

She took her glasses off and looked at me. Her face had lots of wrinkles, and her white hair was wispy thin, but none of that mattered. For just a moment, as she considered my question, all I saw was sadness.

"No. It didn't work. Poor Kitty ended up staying with her host family for a total of five long years. I'm guessing my dear friend threw the spell together in an effort to give me hope. I know she felt bad for me when Kitty was sent away. But there was nothing she could do for me. There was nothing any of us could do but wait. And hope. And wait some more."

This was not the answer I'd wanted, or even expected. I'd imagined a happy homecoming for young Kitty, after her sister did everything she could to bring her home.

But I kept repeating her words over and over, trying to make it sink in.

It didn't work. It didn't work. It didn't work.

"Let me get our tea," she said as she stood. "I'll be right back."

"Would you like some help?" my mum asked.

"That would be lovely, thank you," Sheila said.

After they left, I looked over at my dad and sister. "Try not to be too disappointed," my dad said. "We haven't heard the whole story yet. Maybe there's still a happy ending."

"I hope so," I said softly.

My sister didn't say anything. Just sat there, staring at a pretty painting of a field of red flowers, except for one yellow flower, smack-dab in the middle.

When Mum and Sheila returned with the tea set, Sheila placed the tray on the coffee table and poured each of us a cup. When Sheila sat down again, she picked up right where she'd left off.

"When Kitty came home, I was much older. We all were, of course. It was a difficult adjustment for everyone. In a way, her host family had become her new family. The first few months were especially difficult.

Looking back, I think she must have missed them terribly but didn't want to admit that to us. During any other time, I would have most likely been married and living away from home. But with the war, and all of the young men enlisted, many of us continued to live with our parents."

She stopped to sip her tea. "For a long time, we rarely talked, Kitty and me. It was as if we were strangers. And I suppose, in a way, we were. But then one day, something happened. Something almost . . . magical."

This made me sit up a bit straighter. "What was it?" I asked. "What happened?"

"She woke me early one morning. Very early. Told me, 'Get dressed and come outside. There's something you have to see.' So I did as she said. And when I stepped outside, I saw a sky like I'd never seen before. It was pink and purple and so very lovely. She told me the strange light coming through her window had woken her up. And when she saw it, she'd wanted to share it with me. That was when I reached out and hugged her. And we both started to cry."

"How come?" I asked.

She looked over at my sister, then back at me. "I think for a while it seemed as if we'd lost each other. But we hadn't. Not at all. And I believe that realization made us so happy that tears came with the smiles. You see, no matter what, sisters are forever. Through thick and thin, as the saying goes."

My heart hurt because I wanted a moment like that with my sister. A moment where everything in the past faded away into the colors of the sky and we could just be together. Happily.

I was so lost in my thoughts, wishing and hoping things could be different, it startled me when Alice spoke. "May I ask what happened to Kitty?"

"She eventually married and moved to France," Sheila said as she returned her teacup to the table. "We'd get together every six months or so, and we always had a wonderful time. Sadly, she passed away last year. I'm guessing her daughter didn't realize the letter and photo were inside the compact when she gave it away or sold it." Now she turned to me. "Did you happen to bring it along with you? I'd love to see it."

I looked nervously at Dad, but of course there was nothing he could do. I'd wanted to come here to meet her, even if I knew the subject of the compact might come up. I'd decided in the car to simply be as vague as possible for as long as possible.

"No, I didn't bring it with me," I said. "Sorry."

"Well, that's all right," she said with a smile. "I have my own collection of trinkets that belonged to Kitty. Her daughter was kind enough to send me a box of them. And I kept many of the letters Kitty mailed to me during the war. Those are the real treasures, I suppose."

"That reminds me, I have something else for you." I reached into my bag yet again and pulled out the silver box. "I found this. At Twinings Tea Shop?"

"Ah, yes," she said. I swear there was a happy little twinkle in her eye as she took the box from me. "Thank you. I haven't thought about this for a long, long time." She opened the box and read the poem to herself. Then she asked me, "Were you hoping the spell would work for you?"

It felt kind of silly to admit it, but it felt even more wrong to lie. So I gave her a little nod.

"Well, don't give up hope," she said. "Sometimes magical moments happen when we least expect them.

I'll wish for a bit of magic to find its way to you very soon, all right?"

"Thank you," I told her. "Can I ask you one more question? About the spell? Because I'm curious and it's the only place I haven't visited that's mentioned in the letter."

"Of course," Sheila replied.

"Which cemetery is it referring to?" I asked. "Do you know?"

She gave me a little wink. "That's the most difficult clue of them all, isn't it? I remember being puzzled by that one as well. I believe it's referring to the Nunhead Cemetery. It's a beautiful place with lots of birds. You should visit there sometime, if you're able."

"Maybe I will," I said. And I did want to, mostly because I couldn't deny a small part of me wanted to believe the spell might still work for me, even if it didn't work for Sheila and Kitty.

"Well, I think it's time that we let you get back to your day," Mum said as she pressed her hands down her skirt before standing. "Thank you so very much for letting us visit with you. Phoebe had her heart set on meeting you."

"It was my pleasure," Sheila said. As everyone else stood, she turned to me.

"Did you want these back?" She held out the photo and the letter.

"Oh, no," I said. "I want you to have them."

"Are you sure?" she asked. "Because I'd understand if you wanted to keep them with the compact you purchased."

"That's very kind of you," Dad said, "but it seems fitting to us that they stay with you."

"Definitely," I replied.

"All right, then," Sheila said. "Well, it was wonderful to meet you. Thank you so much for tracking me down to return these items to me."

She showed us to the door, and we all said good-bye. Once outside, Dad smiled and said, "That went well, don't you think?"

"It certainly did," Mum said. "What a nice lady." Neither Alice nor I had said a word. "Are you disappointed about the spell, Phoebe?"

I shrugged. The truth was, I didn't want to admit being disappointed in front of my sister. She'd probably give me a hard time about how immature I'd been to believe it might be real, and I just wasn't in the mood.

"At least you don't have to feel guilty about the compact anymore," Dad said. "She didn't seem to expect it back at all."

"I am relieved about that," I said. "So, where to now? Home?"

"I have an idea," Alice said.

We all looked at her. "Is there somewhere you'd like to go, love?" Mum asked.

"Yes," Alice said. "I'd like to go to Nunhead Cemetery, please."

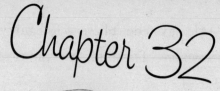

Chapter 32

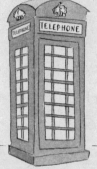

CHIP SHOP: A RESTAURANT THAT SERVES FISH AND CHIPS

I couldn't have been more surprised if she'd said she wanted to fly to Rome and meet the Pope.

"Why do you want to go there?" I asked.

"I think you should complete the spell," she said.

"But—"

Dad didn't let me finish. "I think that's a splendid idea. We'll go there now. And when we're through, we'll stop at a chip shop and have a meal. How's that sound?"

Mum smiled. "A night off from cooking? Sounds wonderful, right, Pheebs?"

"I thought you said I couldn't go?" I asked her. "To the cemetery, I mean."

"That might have been a bit harsh. I was upset at the time. But now, after spending time with Sheila, I love the idea of you following in her footsteps. So I say let's go and check it out."

I was still trying to process what this meant, so all I could manage was, "All right."

In the car, I tried to imagine why Alice would want to do such a thing. Sheila had clearly said the spell didn't work. And besides, even if it did, what did it matter? Alice held all the power in our relationship, didn't she? If we were ever going to be close again, wasn't that all up to her?

When we arrived at the cemetery, Dad parked the car on a street behind it. Across the street was a trail, and that seemed to be the way inside, so we all walked that way. It felt more like a walk in nature than a walk in a cemetery, until we came upon the grave markers.

"What are those people doing over there?" Mum asked, pointing to a crowd.

We all turned and looked. It was a group of all ages—from little kids to elderly people. Some of them had binoculars hung around their necks.

"I bet they're doing some bird watching," Dad said. "With all the trees, I'm sure there are a number of birds to see." He took out his phone and typed something. "Seems there are fifty-two acres here. So lots of space for exploring."

Bird watching in a cemetery? That seemed so strange. Although the place was oddly beautiful. It was almost like something out of a fairy tale. Half lush forest and half ancient grave markers, it was like nothing I'd seen before.

"Peter," my mum said, "I'd love to see the old gothic chapel. I think the girls might like to make their way to the top of the hill to see the view of the city." She turned and looked at us. "Meet us back here in thirty minutes or so? And of course, give a ring if you need anything."

"Uh, sure," I said. It seemed like they wanted Alice and me to be alone. But what I didn't know was if that's what Alice wanted.

Dad pointed us to the trail that would take us to the top of the hill. "The website says there's a stunning view of St. Paul's Dome from up there. Take pictures, please?"

"We will," Alice said.

And with that, they went their way and we went ours. I was surprised at how people strolled along the trails like it was a park. It wasn't a sad place at all. In fact, for a cemetery, it was strange how it was actually bursting with life.

Along the trail, we saw a variety of grave markers, but my favorite was the angel made of stone with her flowing dress and large wings. I pointed to her and said, "Look, she's really good at the sweet angel face." I turned to my sister. "Almost as good as you. That's how I got the compact, you know. By putting on my best sweet angel face."

Alice smiled. "You remember that? That was when Dad let us go off on our own at a flea market for the first time, right?"

"I think so. All I know is I'll never forget that trick. I was so impressed by you and your amazing bartering skills."

We walked along in silence some more, until finally, I couldn't wait any longer. I had to know what she was thinking.

"Alice?"

"Yes?"

"Why did you want to come here?"

"It's hard to explain," she said softly. "Something told me we should."

"Do you mean, like, a voice?"

She chuckled. "No. Not exactly. I mean, something inside of me said we should come here. It just seemed like the right thing to do."

"I get it," I said. "That's the same way I felt about meeting Sheila." We passed a couple of broken crosses. "It's pretty here, isn't it?"

Alice stopped walking and turned to me. "I wanted there to be a happy ending," she blurted out.

I looked at her, confused. "A happy ending to what?"

"To Sheila's story. I wanted Kitty to come home and to be with her family right away. But that didn't happen. And then, when I asked what became of Kitty, it was more bad news. Because she's not here anymore, you know?"

"That was pretty sad."

"Will you write to me?" Alice asked. "When I'm away at university?"

A dad with two young children walked by. One of the kids, a little boy, reminded me a bit of the boy Ned and I had found in the square last week. It took a moment for me to remember his name. Archie. He reminded me of Archie. I kept my eyes on him as I said, "If you'll write to me."

She didn't say anything then. Just turned and followed the family of three up the hill, and so I went, too. When we reached the top, we had to wait for others before we had our turn at the viewpoint.

As we stood there, looking down at the city, St. Paul's standing big and proud in the middle of it all, Alice said, "I don't want it to change."

I looked over at her, and I could see tears pooling up in her eyes.

"What?" I asked.

"I don't want to be the outsider," she said. "The one who's gone. The one who doesn't belong anymore."

"Alice," I said, turning to face her. "Why would you even think that? You'll always belong. Just because you move away doesn't mean you're not one of us anymore. You'll always be one of us."

"Sometimes it just feels like . . . I don't matter as much. Or something."

I couldn't believe what I was hearing. I had complained about feeling exactly the same way to Ned. How was it possible that we had *both* been feeling that way? I mean, she was the sun that shined so brightly that everyone noticed her.

Wasn't she?

Or maybe, sometimes she felt like a dinky star in the night sky, just like me. Maybe we were more alike than I had realized.

I thought of her heartbreak over Justin and how I'd dismissed it completely. And I thought of the compact and how I'd given it away to Ned so easily. Had there been other things I'd done recently to make her feel like she didn't matter? But hadn't she, in her own way, made me feel that way, too?

"I'm sorry I wasn't very understanding about Justin," I told her. "That wasn't nice of me. And I shouldn't have given the compact away. I know that now. But I need to tell you something. Remember when I came into your room to wake you up this morning?"

She smiled. "How could I forget?"

"I actually had something important to tell you."

She stared at me. "You did? What was it?"

"I called Ned and told him I wanted the compact back. That it had been a mistake to give it to him. He's bringing it over later this evening."

She didn't say anything for a moment. "Pheebs, you really did that? You asked for it back?"

"Yes. I made a mistake, and I wanted to make it right. Dad said it should pay for your trips back and forth between London and America, so you don't have to worry about that anymore. I know the scholarships and financial aid won't be sorted out for a while yet, but it's going to be all right, Alice. It really is."

She grinned a big, goofy grin, and then she hugged me. A nice, long hug. "Thank you so much for doing that," she said when we finally pulled away.

"I'm so sorry if I've made you feel like you don't matter," I said. "Because you do. I promise."

She shook her head. "I'm sure it started with me making you feel that way. Sometimes I'm just so jealous of you. And I know I shouldn't—"

I didn't let her finish. "Jealous? Of me? But why?"

"Because you're still a kid. And being a kid is fun! Worry-free. At least, most of the time. When I called you immature about the nail polish name? That was mean. But in that moment, I felt like I wasn't supposed to do things like make up ridiculous names for nail polish colors. I'm heading off to university soon, so I should be much more sophisticated. Even though I don't really want to be. Do you see?"

I shook my head. "Not really. I mean, I thought you were happy to be growing up and moving away?"

"Sometimes I am," she said. "And other times, like I told you earlier, I'm scared to death. And I see you and I wish I didn't have to grow up quite yet." She turned toward the view again. "I know it's completely odd and mixed-up. But that's how my brain is all the time these days."

This was not what I'd expected to hear from her. At all. I thought of little Archie, and how he'd suggested jealousy, and I'd totally blown off the idea. It seemed like Alice's feelings were complicated. Messy. She felt one way one minute and another way the next. But maybe that was understandable. After all, California, or even New York if she ended up there, was a very long way from London.

Perhaps I should have done a better job of imagining what it must be like for her, getting ready to leave home in a few short months. In some ways, it wasn't much different from Kitty going away to live with a different family. I'd felt sorry for her, but why hadn't I felt sorry for my own sister, until now?

Alice continued. "But here's the thing I decided back at Sheila's house. Maybe Sheila and Kitty didn't get the happy ending I wanted for them. But you and me? We certainly can."

"Except, it's not an ending," I said. "It's a beginning."

She smiled. "Yes! A happy beginning. Starting right now. And on to next year, where we'll write each other all the time. Promise?"

It made me laugh. I couldn't believe she actually *wanted* me to stay in touch with her. "Yes! I promise. Do you know why?"

"Why?"

"Because sisters are sisters forever. Through thick and thin."

"Gee, I wonder where I've heard that before," she teased.

We hugged again, and then stared out at the view for another moment, knowing it would have to end soon. There were people behind us, waiting.

"What were you supposed to do here?" Alice asked. "For the spell to be complete?"

"Wave to the birds," I replied.

"Maybe you should do that," she told me. "Here. I'll do it with you."

So we both put our hands in the air and waved all around us. The people waiting probably thought we'd lost our marbles. But I don't think either of us really cared.

Alice pulled out her phone to take a few pictures. After she unlocked it, she tapped a couple of things, then squealed. "Oh my gosh, Phoebe. Justin emailed me back!"

"Finally," I said. "But there isn't time to read it now. We need to go. It'll be time to meet Mum and Dad soon."

So we snapped a few photos and turned to head back down the hill. As we did, Alice looped her arm in with mine.

"When we get home, want to bake something delicious?" she asked.

"I'd love to," I said.

"Maybe we could make cookies so I could send some to Justin."

"All the way to America?"

"Sure. Why not?"

My sister mattered to me. And I now understood how important it was to show her that. "Okay. We'll have to make a double batch then, so there's enough for him and us. Can we tell him to give some of them to Nora, too? I'd hate to leave her out."

"Good idea," she replied.

After we'd walked a while, and came to my favorite stone angel, I said, "Alice?"

"Yes?"

"Do you believe in magic?"

She squeezed my arm a little tighter. "You know what? I think I actually do."

Magic or not, one thing was certain. I hadn't felt that close to my sister in a long time. And it felt positively delightful. Maybe even better than finding a vintage Cartier makeup compact at a flea market in Paris and getting it for dirt cheap.

Yes. Even better than that.

Every city has some hidden magic . . .

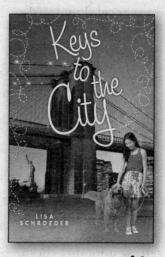

Nora goes on a treasure hunt in Paris. Lindy explores New York City with new friends. Follow them around the world with these unforgettable stories by Lisa Schroeder!

Four Best Friends, One
Charmed Life

Caitlin, Mia, Libby, and Hannah became best friends forever at camp, but now they have to go their separate ways. Luckily, they have a very special charm bracelet to share. As they mail it back and forth, each girl will receive it just when she needs it the most!

Read the latest books!